As Sally neared the pond she caught a glimpse of movement from the corner of her eye. A flash of plaid material and glimmer of skin on the other side of a patch of budding shrubs momentarily surprised her. She slowed her pace and warily walked toward the bushes. Apprehensively, tentatively, Sally leaned over the bushes and spied Nicole in slumbering repose. The swell of Nicole's breasts, coupled with the long smooth tone of her body, transfixed Sally's gaze and rekindled long buried hunger. Pulling her courage around her, she stepped around the thin shrubbery and softly cleared her throat as she emerged on the other side.

Nicole jumped at the sound of the dainty cough and quickly reached for her discarded shirt. Her eyes stared in trepidation, then widened in surprise as she recognized her visitor. Her hand forgot its mission and faltered in its search for her shirt. Amazed and uncertain, she watched Sally move through the rich green shoots of grass. Her light cotton dress moved as it clung to Sally's gentle curves. Nicole was speechless.

LOOKING FOR NAIAD?

Buy our books at
www.naiadpress.com

or call our toll-free number
1-800-533-1973

or by fax (24 hours a day)
1-850-539-9731

Windrow Garden

JANET E. McCLELLAN

THE NAIAD PRESS, INC.
1998

Printed in the United States of America on acid-free paper
First Edition

Editor: Lila Empson
Cover designer: Bonnie Liss (Phoenix Graphics)
Typesetter: Sandi Stancil

Library of Congress Cataloging-in-Publication Data

McClellan, Janet, 1951 –
    Windrow garden / by Janet McClellan.
        p.   cm.
    ISBN 1-56280-216-X   (alk. Paper)
    I. Title.
PS3563.C3413W56   1998
813′.54—dc21   98-13232
                                                                            CIP

To Jane Rule
an extraordinary and gifted
creative writer

About the Author

Janet E. McClellan began a career in law enforcement at the tender age of nineteen. Fresh off the farm and absolutely sure she was invincible, she spent the next twenty-plus years working as undercover narcotic investigator, patrol officer, detective, college professor, prison administrator, and police chief. When not writing mysteries, she spends her time looking for inspiration as she travels and examines the mysteries of Dallas, Texas, Kansas City, Missouri, and Eagles Nest, New Mexico. Her books, *K.C. Bomber*, *Penn Valley Phoenix*, and *River Quay*, featuring Police Detective Tru North, have been published by Naiad Press. The fourth Tru North mystery, *Chimney Rock Blues*, is scheduled for release in 1999.

Life, believe is not a dream
So dark as sages say;
Oft a little morning rain
Foretells a pleasant day.

Charlotte Brontë, "Life"
Stanza 1 (1846)

Chapter 1
Cold Frames & Hotbeds

A cold frame or hotbed is the best and simplest tool whether you are a beginning or avid gardener. Either is a tried and true means for starting plants. Everything stored and grown within may be transferred, at the time appropriate for the particular variety, to the waiting garden. If you use either one of these techniques, you will be rewarded with the earliest appearance of the bounty that comes with the spring.

Tomatoes, cabbage, lettuce, peppers, cucumbers, peas, and flowers of all variety are a few examples of the many things that may be started. All food crops or flowers that need an extended growing season can be initiated in a cold frame or hotbed. If you prefer to start, or wish to experiment with starting, your garden by seed rather than waiting or depending on nurseries, you will be well rewarded by these simple constructions.

A cold frame is a hotbed that does not have the benefit of artificial heat. It has the dual purpose of providing a space for the hardening off of seedlings started in heated protective shelters and or letting them acclimate to local weather conditions before placing them in the garden. A cold frame may also be used to force bulbs or to protect hardy or partially-hardy biennial and perennial flowers. Cold frames may double as hotbeds if you place them in protected places and if they face the south and have water, heat, good drainage, and location where you can keep an eye on your prospects.

You may construct an old-fashioned hotbed or cold frame by digging a pit twenty-four to thirty inches deep. The finished, full size of the frame should provide enough space to meet your needs. A minimum of five-by-six feet to a maximum of six-by-eight feet is recommended for the average gardener. Construct the wooden frame to fit in the pit so that the walls extend above the soil line about eight to ten inches on the low side and fourteen to sixteen inches on the high side.

Note: Place the high side of the protected hotbed against a building and face it so that the sunlight pervades the interior. Make the frame full (four sided). The high side against the building should be lined with plastic; the low side should be unlined to allow for drainage. Fill and mound the outside of the framed pit with soil. Place the mounded soil against the outside walls. This provides additional insulation and protection for the tender seedlings and plants you are trying to nurture.

In the pit from which the soil has been removed, place eighteen to twenty-four inches of manure. It is strongly recommended that you use manure from horses or cows and that you add straw or other natural, biodegradable litter. Cover the manure with six inches of soil. Water the contents of the hotbed or cold frame thoroughly.

Enclose the top of the cold frame or hotbed with an easy-to-remove cover of framed glass, Plexiglas, or plastic to keep in the heat and the natural moisture condensation that will form. Make the framed cover light and easy to lift or prop up so that you can get at the seedlings.

In about two weeks the manure in the hotbed will begin to ferment and generate enough heat for the seedlings. Do not plant until then. Fresh manure is too harsh, and seedlings will perish from the lethal soil. Cold frames may take a little longer for the proper fermentation to take place. Seedlings may be started in the house or the outdoor planters after you have finished the construction of the hotbed or cold frame. Paper mesh cups or any other kind containing a planting soil and the seeds you wish to start may be placed inside in a south-facing window. The sun or, in a less temperate region, the constant heat of a common lamp will aid your new plants in getting started.

Planting seeds in the cold frame or hotbed takes some care. Mark off shallow rows, about four to eight inches apart in the prepared bed and sprinkle the seeds. Do not overfill; four to eight seeds per inch of row is sufficient.

After the young plants emerge from the soil, you will want to thin the plants to one plant per every two inches. New growth will need room to expand. Firm the soil over the seedlings and water very gently, keeping in mind that these are young growing things. Make sure to mark each row with an empty container of seeds or other marker. Nothing is more disturbing than losing your place. Allow six to eight weeks before transplanting the seedlings to the garden or field. Refer to the instructions on the packages (the ones you saved) that give the proper planting depth and germination temperatures for the seedlings.

With some attention, time, and tenderness, you will be rewarded for your efforts.

Groundwork

Sally Windrow straightened her aching back and leaned against the hoe. She cast her eyes northward to the line of growing gray clouds. A woolen scarf wrapped close to her auburn hair and tightly around her neck protected her from gusts of wind and the thawing winter's chill. The farmhand work clothes she had chosen for the day's labors camouflaged her full, work-firmed body. She was practical, pragmatic, and unafraid of hard work. Although she would deny it, she was a risk taker. Her practical, conservative temperament shared a curious lack of recognition that she, like other farmers, gambled with their lives by betting against the unpredictabilities of nature.

She stood on the southeast corner of the modest house that had once been her parents' home. Her father had built the house on the farm shortly after his return from Vietnam. Before he'd managed to use his GI bill, and until Sally was five, they had lived in one of the two cottages his father had built for the hired hands. He had built their home with timber from their own woods. He'd milled the lumber himself and then sold the small lumber saw for the money he needed for a poured concrete basement. White vinyl siding, trimmed out in black on the frames and windows, now covered the former clapboard. It was the same rambling three-bedroom ranch house Sally had grown up in except for the expanded living room she'd added to accommodate her new fireplace. Her daughter claimed her old bedroom. Sally used her parents' bedroom for her home office, and she had laid claim to the larger spare bedroom as her own.

From where she stood at the side of the house, she could view the wide sweep of the five-acre clutch of barns, restaurant with its parking lot, hired-hand housing and cottages, outbuildings, machinery sheds, sheltered greenhouses, and animal shelters with their fenced pens. It was the working nucleus of her farming domain. It was the heart of what her life had returned to, where she regained a peace with herself and a sense of belonging again.

The farm had changed during the seventy-five years her family had owned it. Her grandparents had first secured a toehold in the land, and with hard work they let their roots sink deep to secure their futures. Each generation had added something — barns, outbuildings, animal sheds, tool and equipment sheds, and garages for all manner of vehicles. In the forties, Grandfather Windrow had planted new orchards of nut-bearing trees, added strategically arranged beehives, and constructed the two large, glass-paneled nurseries.

In the sixties, Sally's father added several small cottages and converted an old barn into a triplex for the live-in hired help and their families. The living quarters for the hired help had been her mother's idea. Her mother had reasoned, and rightly so, that good help was hard to find and keep without offering more stability than mere wages. Her mother's insight had changed Windrow Garden from a family concern into a small community.

As she looked northward, Sally could see, sense, and smell the coming changes in the weather. The unusual, teasingly balmy last days of winter would shift again, and not for the better. What had passed for warmth had made it possible to begin to prepare the machinery for spring chores. The sky and rising winds foretold the possibilities of cold or freezing rain. A typical March prank. Neither would be welcome. If the freeze did come, Sally knew that winter might not loosen its hold completely until April was well underway. Bad weather now would slow and make difficult the work that she and her staff needed to complete before one of the busiest times of the year.

Spring required the preparation of the land, fertilizing, disking, sowing, and transplanting the readied seedlings. Everything took time, and delays would produce uncertainties for the intended truck-farm crops. Farm creatures might suffer and reduce their gifts. Chickens would lay fewer eggs, cows would produce less milk, and ewes would have hard birthing. Everything responded to the weather.

Weather was the conversation, concern, and consternation of all who depended on the land. It focused the attention, shaded the mood, and tightened the stomach in dismay. Her father had once told Sally that the reason people in the Midwest spent so much time talking about the weather was because there was so much of it. He'd meant change, and change in weather was the constant of farming life. She'd sought stability and comfort in every other aspect of her life that she could manage. It had not done that much good. When the cancer had taken her husband, she'd discovered that change came in more forms than weather and often with more devastating results.

The weather threatened now. Sharp, gusting breezes danced about her in warning. A northern blow was coming, and she felt her irritation rise. She'd hoped and prayed for a lasting and gentle end of winter, but the dark cloud bank made her realize she'd been hoping against her own better wisdom of Kansas. Cold rain and tiny pellets of ice and snow might come from those clouds. If it did, it would confine her to the house or tiny roadside restaurant and the tasks she might manage there. It was not an idea she relished. She preferred the outdoors. Fresh air, even cold fresh air, was stimulating. She'd grown accustomed to it, and she felt more in her element outdoors than in the confines of the restaurant she'd built.

She squinted. Fine lines traced their minute, sun-etched paths from the corners of her green eyes. Sally knew they were there, but she wasn't bothered that they'd begun to show at thirty-two. She'd earned them. They might have begun in the lonely hours and years that had passed since her life had been unaccountably rearranged by death. For her part, Sally believed the lines had begun to arrive with her return to the sun, wind, and rain that farmwork exposed her to. It did not matter. As far as she was concerned, they were a small price for the life that brought her heart joy again.

She'd come home to the farm three years ago to become the third generation to own and operate the farm. It had been something she never thought she would do. But come back she did, six months after her husband's death. She and her daughter returned after Sally graduated from a culinary school. Sorrow and the need to put distance between them and their old life brought them home. They arrived with a small faith in the certainty of the changing of the Midwestern seasons, the hope for a reaffirmation in life, and time. Hope and work had sustained them as the shock of their loss slowly receded.

Her mother had been so pleased when Sally brought her own contribution and the fourth generation to the farm with her. Sally's daughter, Gwynn Marian, named for both grandmothers, was twelve going on twenty-five. A miniature replica of Sally's youthful, wiry self, Gwynn Marian had initially been appalled at being transplanted into the country life. Bright, gregarious, flamboyant, and a serious tomboy, she quickly acclimated. She discovered the freedom of space, the liberty of rolling hills, the secrets of wooded tracts, and the opportunity of heady speed that her pony provided. When not engaged in pursuits across the two sections of acreage deeded to her mother, Gwynn Marian would read, surf the monitored Internet, and entertain herself with the affordable luxury of cable television. A little loner, transplanted from the urban environs and progressive educational systems of Dayton, Ohio, Gwynn Marian found her local classmates little more than amusing. She tolerated them but found it hard to take them seriously as friends, academic competition, or athletic contenders. She missed her father. She'd try to remember his kindness, interest in her life, and the confidence he'd provided. In the three years since his death, his face had faded from sharp memory to a faint shadow renewed only by disheartening curious reminders offered in photos.

Sally glanced at the hotbeds and cold frames where they lay huddled against the south sides of her house, nearby greenhouses, and barns. In two to four weeks, the cold frames and hotbeds would become the first homes to a variety of vegetables for the gardens used by the people and families on farms and in towns throughout the county. She and the other hands on the farm would begin sowing the vegetables that needed the greatest length of time before transplanting. Sally was in a hurry for spring and wanted to see the new shoots working their way through the soil.

It was very different from the farm her grandfather had bought. His original garden plots had grown from feeding his small family to supplying the local farmer's market and grocery and health food stores throughout the surrounding metropolitan area.

From small and modest beginnings, the truck farm had grown under the careful and watchful hands of her family for seventy years. It had become a family corporation of truck farming, greenhouses, and Sally's addition of a restaurant featuring home cooking and scrumptious cheesecakes served in the house that had once belonged to her grandparents. The sign for Windrow Garden Restaurant faced the two-lane blacktop. Its reputation, if not the location, drew people from the surrounding small communities of Leavenworth, Lansing, Bashor, Tonganoxie, and even a few strays from both Kansas Cities snuggled against the banks of the Missouri River.

Two meals a day, Wednesday through Sunday, and all the cheesecakes that Sally's imagination and available ingredients might provide were offered. The meals were simple. You got whatever was the one main fare prepared for each sitting. Every day it was something new, but there was only one choice coming out of the small converted kitchen, and that was whatever Sally had planned.

Soups, hot breads, potatoes mashed or fried, salad, and cheesecakes were staples. Even a vegetarian could thrive on the fresh or home-canned creations she prepared in the kitchen. The main meal was always the surprise and the point of basic culinary interest for her guests. The Midwestern taste for meat and potatoes received a jolt through the nontraditional glories she packed into the chief course. Fish, fowl, beef, lamb, or pork, but only one. One drawn and created with heart and mind bent on pleasing the eye, filling the inner void, and titillating the tongue. One at a time. It saved money in preparation and ensured full use of what she'd provisioned. The day's fare was available to paying guests and farmhand alike. There was always enough but not so much that profit was thrown away.

The idea of converting her grandparents' house into a restaurant had seemed a good idea at the time. Lately, however, Sally had begun to wonder if she'd bitten off more than she might chew. Her mother, Gwynn, had encouraged her in her entrepreneurial spirit and happily moved to the nearby town of Leavenworth, Kansas, to be closer to other retired friends. Sally had no difficulty securing a loan for her project. The farm and its long legacy had been more than enough collateral. Legacy or not, money had been a little tight over the last year. There were resident hired hands to pay and new restaurant staff to compensate. The combined operations made money, paid the bills, and provided for her and her daughter's needs. It had taken most of Sally's time and much work to get the restaurant operating as a quasiprofitable venture and to keep the farm prosperous. She tried never to steal time from her daughter. Instead, she stole it from herself. Her social life had been reduced to the hub of her farm.

She put time, heart, and soul into the farm and restaurant. She had not forsaken love. Sally simply put it out of her mind. She did not allow herself time to think or do anything other than work. When she did think of love, she conveniently fortified her resolve to ignore her heart's whispered yearnings by attending to a project until the idea evaporated under the exertions.

She would tell herself that she had her daughter, her work, and the farm. She tried to let that be enough. Sometimes it was. She could toil in the restaurant with staff or labor in the field with farmhands and could go for days without feeling lonely. Her mind knew there was no other place in the world she would rather be, no other thing that she would rather be doing, and no life she would rather live. Still, her heart's regret was that her satisfaction came at the price of being alone.

Sally stretched her back against the awkward strain her tasks had caused her, frowned again at the low rolling clouds, and turned back to her work. There was always work to be done on the farm. And in Kansas, spring would have its typical struggle to take hold of the world again.

She dropped her hoe, turned back to the wheelbarrow, and lifted out another shovel of dirt to cover the hotbed's layer of manure. She automatically glanced at the untreated wood of the hotbed, checking it for weathering and rot. She never used treated wood. It would have leaked chemicals into the soil and tainted the seedlings she intended to grow. There would be no taint in her organic farm. However, she would have to repair the plastic sheeting on the framed lids. Even thickest clear plastic could not last through more than two seasons. Wind, weather, storms, and accidental rips were part of their lot.

Bending to her work, she smiled to herself as she remembered it was Monday. The restaurant would not open for business again until Wednesday. Her daughter would not be home from school until almost four o'clock. She figured she had enough time to do some things for the farm and a few things for herself. She was glad that she would remain mostly undisturbed for two whole days. In the evening she would ask her daughter how her day had been. Wednesday it would be back to the food preparation for lunches and suppers, except Sunday when only a late lunch would be served to the churchgoing folks.

Thirty minutes later, after she had managed to put the finishing touches on the hotbeds by making sure that the warming bulbs were working, Sally walked to the old barn to look for a roll of plastic sheeting for the framed lids. Lost in her own thoughts as she approached the huge double doors, a rumbling collapsing sound from the interior startled Sally. Just as suddenly, an alarmed scream erupted from inside the barn and sent a chill down her spine. She grabbed hold of the large wooden handle and jerked the door open with all her might. Inside, the windowless gloom of the old barn and the billowing dust made her blink and stumble against a scattered drift of hay on the floor. A second scream came from the darkened interior, quickly followed by the pained cursing from a man's terrified throat. Sally dashed past the machinery and ran as fast as she could toward the sound.

At the back of the barn, near the corn combine, Sally found Bill Cornweir pinned under a pile of hay bales. As Sally rushed to his side, Cornweir raised himself under the green avalanche and tried to use his broad shoulders and thick arms to move the hay away.

"Are you all right?" Sally asked, kneeling next to the stricken man.

"I can't get out..." he said and collapsed against his exertions.

"Lie still. You don't know what damage you'll do."

"Can't seem to...breathe good," he complained as beads of perspiration flecked his forehead. The false heat was an odd contrast to the billowing breaths of steam coming from his mouth in the cold barn. His chest heaved against the weight of the bales that held him and made his breath labor more.

Sally rose from where she'd knelt and grabbed the first bale she laid her hands on. She lifted and jerked it up and away from him in panicked motion. As she raised the bale from his body, he tried to move but screamed again as something seemed to tear inside him. The scream panicked Sally. With the bale in midair, she jerked involuntarily at the sound of Bill's shriek. She toppled backward with the bale.

"Damn it, Bill, I said lie still."

"Ah, lassie...it hurts," he moaned, and sank to the floor again.

"Wait. I've got to get help. Don't move!" Sally ordered, scrambling to her feet as she turned to run.

Outside she ran toward the houses and yelled as loud as she could for anyone who might hear. Heads emerged from the greenhouses, and two men came running toward her. In the next instant Carl Marmer and Jake Grimes were at her side. They had been fertilizing and watering the new berry bushes when

Sally called for help. Carl was a tall lanky man in his late forties. He'd run ahead of the sixty-five-year-old Jake and reached Sally first.

"Bill's in the barn, hurt. Stay with him," she said as she dashed past them. "Don't touch him, the bales, or anything. And don't let him move! I'm going to call an ambulance." She raced past them to the tack room and the phone on the desk. Fear thundered in her ears. She did not like the graying paleness on Bill's face when he'd slumped back to the floor of the cold barn.

Twenty minutes later the paramedics arrived, escorted by a sheriff's department officer. The barn had filled with Carl's wife, Martha, and the two younger male part-time workers. They'd seen people running to and from the barn and had come to offer whatever help they could. There had not been much to do but worry. The farmstead workers were milling about nervously, not knowing what to do, or taking turns as they tried to keep Bill conscious and still. The paramedics found Sally sitting next to Bill, holding his hand, and trying to say encouraging words to him. They examined Bill, stabilized him, carefully rolled him onto a flat-board restraint, secured it, and carried him into the ambulance.

Sally motioned to the ambulance driver, her eyebrow raised in question.

"Too early to tell," the driver said, understanding the silent inquiry. "Broken leg for sure, some ribs by the way he's acting. Might be some internal injuries as well. We won't really know till they get a look at him at the hospital," she said as she climbed up into the cab of the ambulance.

"Jake, go with him. Make sure they know he has insurance," Sally said, waving to the elderly man. "I'm going to call his fiancée. She'll want to know."

"Sure thing, Sally girl," the old man said as he scrambled inside the unit and sat next to the attending paramedic.

Sally felt a deep, sinking feeling swirling in the pit of her stomach as the ambulance drove away with her mechanic and right-hand man. She depended on him. As the farm's ten-year veteran at fifty-five, Cornweir was the backbone of the farm and a respected member of their little, rolling-hill community. No other hand had done as much as he to keep things running and running smoothly. He was the glue that held the farm together. It would take a long time for his injuries to heal.

"Fine thing," she said to herself, shaking her head. "I'm acting like I'm the one who got injured. Ungrateful," she muttered to herself as she walked toward her house. She made sure everyone who worked for her was insured for injury and covered by medical insurance. She'd done everything she could think of to protect the farm and the businesses. But now she heard her own head talking to her like she and the farm were the only things that counted. She did not like the message. She could not, would not desert him, but she would need to temporarily replace him. The business of farming had to go on. If it didn't, neither she nor anyone else would have the farm to call their own. That was unthinkable.

Chapter 2
Grounds for Growing

A compost heap is the oldest form of recycling. As the art of composting is a matter of patience, you will need to create the heaps four to six months in advance of application on the garden. However, rapid composting can be done during warm weather if the pile contents have been shredded or ground into finer pieces, mixed together with manure, and placed in a container lined with plastic. This method does not require the turning or mixing as in the slower technique. In summertime, the shredded, mixed pile should be available for use in two to three weeks. During the cooler times of the year, it would take five to six weeks before the mixture would be available.

Locate a compost heap in an area where water does not stand. Drainage is important. Although it is possible to accumulate compost in a loose heap, it is best to make an enclosure. Different types of materials for construction may be used if the heap is placed above ground. Constructing a compost heap above ground is easier than laboriously digging a pit. Unmortared cement blocks, bricks, scrap lumber or permanent enclosures of redwood or cypress, and woven wire or wood slats are preferred construction materials. Lining the wire or fencing with tough plastic will speed the compost decomposition.

For slow composting, put soil or sand in the bottom of the pile in layers two to three inches thick. Add a similar thickness of organic materials. If the organic materials are coarse, use six to eight inches of material instead. If the materials are finely chopped such as grass clippings, use the first method. Then add a two- to three-inch layer of manure. Manure provides nutrients for the growth of microorganisms that are necessary if the compost pile is to do its work. Repeat the layering process until the container is full. Make sure to water frequently as you put in the layers. Do not, however, drown the layers as you place them in the container. *Discretion* is the byword here.

Note: The top of the pile will need to be indented, or be slightly lower in the center than at the sides. The dent or dish will allow rainfall to soak in rather than to run off. High temperatures generated in the compost pile will require that the pile be moistened once a week if dry weather prevails. A dry compost pile overheats, works too rapidly, and loses its nutrient substances. Compost may be used as soil enhancement, fertilizer for the garden, mulch for shrubs, or topdressing for the lawn.

In two to three weeks, if all goes well, the pile will shrink and sink. If not, you can loosen the contents of the pile to allow for greater aeration or water it if it is too dry. The pile should be checked for strong ammonia or other offensive odors, which are sure signs that things are not progressing as intended. Overwatering or an imbalance of the mix of materials causes offensive odors. In four or five weeks the pile should be hot deep inside. At the end of three or four months, the pile should be half its original size. The compost should have the odor of moldy leaves or, better yet, an earthy rich aroma, and will be dark, moist, and ready to use

Compost added to the garden provides important nutrients to the soil for successful garden projects. It is no small coincidence that the words *nutrients, nutrition,* and *nurture* are derived from the Latin root word that means *to feed*. Everything that lives must be fed what it lacks in order to survive and to flourish.

Groundwork
Master Sergeant Nicole Jeager tossed the last of her personal items into the jump seat of her blue

dually truck. The covered bed was already full to bursting. As she slammed the truck door, she realized that for the first time in twenty years she did not know what she was going to do with the rest of her day. Worse, she did not know what she was going to do with the rest of her life. She looked up at the cold, gray sky and realized that it looked as melancholy as she felt. March, having come in like a lion, was trying to leave the same way. The temperament of the weather suited her. It seemed fitting that the weather would be as disagreeable as her attitude about being forced out of the Army. She did not want to leave, but she knew it was time to go. The morning maneuvers were beginning, people were on their way to their assignments, and she was discarded. A last tour of duty had been cut short, and there was no one arriving to see her off. Rumors were thick, and she was barely escaping unscathed. She would do it alone and ignore the averted eyes of those with whom she'd worked during her last year. It would be the last time she set foot on the government's property at Fort Leonard Wood — or Fort Lost in the Woods, as it was called by those who served there.

What do civilians do? she wondered as she stood outside the noncommissioned personnel quarters. Unconsciously, she ran a hand through her thick black hair and brushed back the stray strands from her dark eyes. Proud and tall, her firm form almost sagged under the weight of the outlandish question she thought she would not have had to answer for a long time. She had intended to retire when she was fifty-five. Her leaving now was fifteen years shy of her goal. Her old plans had included staying in until she'd given the Army thirty-five years. That intention would have provided her with a retirement equal to a hundred percent of her monthly pay. But now, a bit over forty, she'd only served the minimum and barely escaped with her pride, reputation, pension, and honorable discharge intact. Her reputation on the base had been shadowed but not swallowed by rumor. She was escaping not a moment too soon. Still, she was reluctant to go. She had given the Army everything it had ever asked for. It had been the only place where she felt respected and valued. It was one more home she didn't have anymore.

She'd joined the Army at eighteen. Every day since then, her life had been planned, orchestrated, and directed by the needs of an organization she'd felt pride in belonging to. For twenty-two years, two months, and five days, the only thing that she had ever been required to respond had been *Yes, sir*, or *Yes, ma'am, I'd be delighted.* Nothing short of direct compliance, assured competence, and timely delivery had been required of her or the soldiers she supervised. She'd given willingly and had served proudly.

For the longest time, but not as long as she wanted, she had hidden in an olive-drab closet in the Army, which became a comforting certainty, a family, and a career. Her enlistment had been a necessary escape from the poverty and hopelessness she'd known as a child.

She had fled the drudgery of the farm life she'd been born into in upper Michigan. She had fled a childhood filled with hard labor, too many mouths at the table, too little food, and parents worn down from the tribulations of scraping by. Poor little half-breeds. That was what the locals had called Nicole and her siblings. Her parents were from different nations. One white and one part-Pottowattomie. Removed from her mother's people and the reservation in Wisconsin, struggling alone in the harsh northeast, the family could not find the ends everyone else worked to make meet. The oldest of seven, tall for her age, and good with her hands, she had become the repository of all the responsibilities her parents could or would no longer assume. Being required from the time she was ten to be responsible for the children, to work in the fields, and to help her father in repairing the equipment had made her accountable beyond her years. The long years of struggle had made her father a hard, bitter man who spent a lot of time reading from the Bible. He began sermonizing to his silent wife and bewildered children. He closed the doors of their house to the outside world and harbored secret fears and suspicions against their infrequent visitors.

Nicole's mother tried to shelter her from her father's growing anger, but she could not protect her all the time. The anger became distance as he heaped more responsibilities on her for the success or failure of the small farm. She had wanted to help him be proud again, to help him make his dreams work, and to chase the growing fear from his haunted eyes.

As the years passed, the whispering of neighbors changed from taunting speculation about why he'd married his olive-skinned wife to a real and alarmed concern for his sanity. He began to hide in the house, shunning work for fear he'd have to meet those who ridiculed him and his life.

Nicole took his place in the outside world at

fourteen. She had been relegated to a position of being the third parent and extra farmhand. She'd found a natural calling as the one who would defuse a crisis, the one who could bring light and laughter back into a situation. A quick smile, a rephrasing of the obtuseness of nature or difficulties kept the family moving and breathing even down their hard road. It was necessary work. What first was survival became habit in time.

During her senior year in high school, Nicole had begun dreaming of escape. Her mother encouraged and nurtured her dreaming, urging her to find a way to make her own way in the world. The dream had grown into a real possibility during senior career week and her introduction to an Army recruiter. Senior girls had not been invited to the presentation of the military recruiters. She and the other girls had been shuttled off to occupational vendors touting secretarial schools and nursing academies and a few colleges attempting to attract future teachers. She had heard the military recruiters talking as she lingered in the hallway between her assigned sessions. She heard them telling about enlistment bonuses, faraway travel, and the excitement of adventure, special duty, freedom, and independence. It had been simple. She would have the opportunity to make something of herself in the Army. Something beyond her bitter, hardscrabble adolescence and beyond her endless days of backbreaking toil.

Nicole had lain in wait and collared the tall, broad-shouldered man in the dark green uniform as he left the building. He was impressive, and Nicole hesitated. Then she gushed out her interest to him as she stared at the march of yellow service stripes sewn on the forearm of his sleeve. He responded to her interest with enthusiasm and a hint of amusement in his voice. He did not try to diminish or belittle her obvious sincerity. He handed her forms and brochures and told her where to find the recruiting station should the allure of his profession remained undiminished.

Three months later, before graduation, and two days after her eighteenth birthday, she enlisted. Having lied to her parents for the first and last time in her life, she had begged them to let her go to an away basketball game with friends. She told them she would stay overnight with teammates and let them know later what the big city had been like. It was a fib, a tiny untruth, and a direct defiance of her father's orders never to stray from the path he harangued and preached about. The lie took her to an induction station. It took her down the corridors of physical, psychological, and vocational examinations the Army performed on her. It matched her with her interests, her natural mechanical abilities, her hopes, desires, and dreamed-of opportunities. A way out.

On graduation night, instead of joining the noisy celebrants in all-night parties, Nicole ran down the streets of the little town and boarded the midnight bus for basic training in Georgia.

During the first week of basic, she'd written her parents, trying to explain to them why she had made the decision she had. She sent money and promised she would send more every payday. She tried to tell them why she'd left, why she wanted a different life, why she had to leave. On every day of the twelve weeks of basic training, and in every letter she mailed, Nicole asked for their blessings.

When all the letters were returned to her, unopened, she never wrote her parents again. She contacted a bank in the town close to home and enlisted a bank officer to open an account for her mother. Nicole had made him promise to tell her mother about the account but to keep it a secret from her father and to make sure neither her parents nor siblings would ever go completely without. From that time forward, Nicole sent a quarter of her pay to the bank. When she finished basic training as a corporal, she found a home in the Army but had lost her family.

As the years passed, she continued to send birthday cards and holiday cards at the appropriate times of the year. She avoided courting the disappointment and the pain of their disapproval by never again including a return address on the envelope.

Fourteen years later when the bank sent word that her parents had died, they sent along a notarized balance of the savings account she'd contributed to. The contributions and accumulated interest had remained all but untouched. There was no word from her brothers and sisters. All the cords of her life had been cut, and they dangled forever out of reach.

Nicole grew up in the Army. She'd made her decision and, like the good soldier she was, pursued the idea of being the best that she could be. Nicole learned how to repair, overhaul, and fix any jeep, truck, or car the Army ever bought or invented. She rose from mechanic to vehicle pool manager in her new family. She was paid, proud, and dedicated. Nicole felt securely comfortable with the life she'd chosen, except for one tiny issue. The Army did not like queers. As supportive of and pleased with her as they were, the bias remained. The Army continued to promote her and give her glowing evaluations, but it would have all stopped if her superiors had known or suspected her other life decision.

They would have stopped the praise and begun an unwavering process toward dishonorable discharge. Ever wary, she pursued her chosen lifestyle with the same commitment with which she cheerfully repaired vehicles.

The Army's policy made for a stinking pile of attitude in the service. It was a wrong that was not going to get fixed. The military held the sad, bad philosophy that homosexuals were incapable of serving honorably. Fear and loathing were leisure pursuits of peacetime. During wartime, everyone had the same and equal opportunity to be among the quick or the dead. Prejudice only raised its ugly, ravaging head during peacetime when the Army turned carnivorous and ate its young.

For more than twenty years, Nicole gave the Army everything she had, except what and who she wanted to have on her time off. The Army got all the work but never the center of her heart. That she reserved for the ladies. There had been some ladies! Tall and short, full and thin, foreign and native to the United States, ladies all. Each was left behind for the next duty assignment.

The Army had given her several gifts of mixed blessing. Most mixed of all was the realization that she could not sustain a long-term relationship. She never tried. Each fair bounty of womanly delights came into her life and exited with the same understanding that possessed Nicole. All things that had been would end with the duration of the tour. It had not been what she had chosen or wished to have happen. Rather, it had been just one more set of facts she'd taken as truth in the Army.

She was not alone. Others like her accepted or dealt with the situation as fact and rule. Some did not, but those were the people most likely to be exposed and disposed of at the Army's earliest opportunity. Disposal was the best one could hope for in the Army. Horror stories of men and women doing serious prison time in a military disciplinary barracks were real and not the stuff of paranoid fantasies.

She worked with other brothers and sisters in the closet of the Army. They worked shoulder to shoulder, keeping their lives and loves separate from their duties. No less and more often than not, they were much more extraordinarily circumspect than their heterosexual counterparts. They were less likely to make indiscriminate lunges of flirtation in and among the ranks. The military code of justice was an oxymoron.

Up until recently, Nicole had managed to secure her pension and save her stripes from the snooping of the investigation division. Then things took a different turn, and the Army began to turn its attention to Nicole.

The security of her world was given a crashing blow in late February. A little too drunk, a bit too sure of herself, and way too quick to bed the fine young flirting corporal from South Carolina, and Nicole had almost got caught. The whole episode had been a dangerously close call. The provost marshal had been watching the young corporal for weeks. Twenty-two and fearless, the young South Carolinian played hide-and-seek with the military authorities regarding her sexual preferences. Flamboyant and foolhardy, she risked her own stripes as well as Nicole's.

Tiring of her impertinent games, the provost marshal scooped up the corporal after discovering her during one of their stakeouts around the gay bars in Saint Louis, Missouri, where she and Nicole frequently went during long days of leave. It had been a don't-ask-don't-tell-be-damned coordinated effort with local authorities. The Army, true to form, utilized eager, slinking homophobes of its own to enter and stake out the world of alternatives. The provost marshal's office held the corporal for thirty-six hours. Between being grilled about her associations and assignations, she was allowed five hours sleep. The Army hadn't cared if the names she offered were known, suspected, best guesses, or lies. When she faltered, they gave her a complete and terrifying case illustration of life in the disciplinary barracks — her life as it could have been for the next five to ten years. The corporal relented, dissolved under their harangue, and agreed to look at a list of names they offered her for her failing memory. She melted under the promise of a general discharge if only she would give names. A lot of names.

Nicole had begun to hear the rumblings from a long way off. Years of keeping her ears close to the ground, going along to get along, and granting favors that only a master sergeant might provide paid off one time in a big way. The last gift of information came from an officer and gentlewoman Nicole had met years before. The officer had information access, concerns of her own, and fond memories of a youthful, more pleasant billeting with Nicole.

The officer, affecting interest in the progress of repairs of her staff car, had come to the vehicle pool. While engaging Master Sergeant Jeager in a discussion about carburetors and timing devices, the lieutenant colonel dropped the word. She was safe from the latest round of witch hunting. As assistant post commander, she was in charge of the investigations and rendered an old friend a last act of kindness.

Reluctantly, Nicole took the officer's advice, deciding that discretion was the better part of valor. She filed for early retirement. Minimum twenty plus netted Nicole a little over half of her former salary. A dishonorable discharge would have cost her everything and very likely her freedom.

Nicole walked to the driver's side of her truck, feeling awkward in her atypical civilian attire of jeans and jacket. She carefully checked the discharge certificate for sly, cryptic lettering and numbers that would have hinted any innuendo of sexual indiscretion or suspicion the Army might have wanted to share with future employers other than what the boldly printed HONORABLE DISCHARGE confirmed. She saw no implication other than conclusion of twenty years of straightforward service. The Army had not tainted her service with cryptic allegations of lesbianism. She would not be barred from future government or security-related employment. She would not have to be subjected to any level of federal or bureaucratic gaze of comprehension when someone reviewed her DD 214.

At forty, she was a long way from a home she could never go back to and a much longer way from knowing what to do with the rest of her life.

Nicole rolled the discharge into a tube and tossed it in the backseat of the cab. She walked to the garage next to her old housing unit to retrieve her personal sets of tools. She shifted uncomfortably in her civilian clothes. During her years of service she'd come to depend on wearing green every day and not worrying what to wear for what occasion. The idea of having to worry about what to wear for work, if she should find any, sent strange chills down her spine and ripples of anxiety up to a new level as she moved the last of the toolboxes to the truck.

Nicole climbed into the truck and let the diesel engine continue to hum its well-maintained tune. It rumbled and purred under her touch as she headed down the street and through the post gates for one last time. Out on the highway, she began to wonder if it would be practical to simply take a long vacation and spend some of her stockpiled savings trying to get used to being free. Her monthly retirement checks would give her a fair income. Nothing fancy, nothing indulgent, but it was everything she would need.

Going nowhere fast, Nicole drove down Interstate 44 to Springfield and then meandered through the rolling hills and bluffs toward Kansas City, Missouri. The miles and hours fell away under the wheels of her truck like the slow awakening from a bad dream. She drove farther north, along the river as night settled in.

As she crossed the line into Kansas north of Kansas City, Missouri, she shuddered involuntarily as she drove past the entrance to Fort Leavenworth. She willed her eyes back on the road and tried to control the angry rise in her throat. It had been a long day. She was tired. She couldn't remember the roads she'd been traveling. Images of the life she lost howled in her head, held her mind, and cast an oppression more substantial than the heavy cloud cover of winter.

A tenseness crept along her back and down her arms. The eight-hour drive and angry congestion in her heart had taken their toll. As she braked to a stop at the corner of Tenth Street and Broadway in the small, historic military town of Leavenworth, Kansas, she spied a café sign. She decided it was time for more coffee if she was going to keep up her driving pace much longer. She wanted to think. She had begun to realize that her driving had taken her off on a generalized northerly route, as though she intended to wind her way home to Michigan. The full impact and realization of how desperately lost she was emotionally hit her like a mallet. There was no home anymore, and there seemed to be no place to find refuge. She sat in the cab of the truck and looked at the blinking lights of the café and knew she would have to make another decision. The idea of traveling west intrigued her but would have to be examined in the clearer light of day.

Inside the café, Nicole deliberated about flirting with the dark-eyed waitress, but she decided to keep her ideas and eyes on the coffee cup instead. While sitting and wondering if she should order breakfast, a discarded newspaper caught her eye. Nicole reached for it and, without intending to, began reading through the help wanted section.

Chapter 3
Lay of the Land

The Midwest was the last region of the United States to be imprinted with the American fervor for the organization of space. This part of the Midwest, having been passed up earlier as being a great inland desert, was ignored during the initial movement toward the more fertile western coasts and mountains. Having received the fervor last, the Midwest has retained it the longest. The square homestead of the pioneer, sitting as it does in a corner of a square section, continues to reflect the patterns of the contemporary township.

These geometric patterns are modified and softened only by the rolling terrain of woods, valleys, and streams. A tendency toward grids sometimes makes a startling effect on a curving landscape. However, there is never a good argument against functional beauty. Improving conservation or enhancing production is never an excuse for ignoring or eliminating natural beauty.

In the earliest years of homesteading, women carried young trees from their origins as they traveled to their future homes. They foresaw a need to make their homesites attractive and livable. They had visions of the richness of light and form that they did not forsake.

The most significant dimension of landscaping is time, and time is never static. Trees bring art to landscaping and take nature's own time to grow, mature, and to finally give back to the earth again. People who plant trees have a greater comprehension of life's continuity, succession, and connectedness. Trees generally last longer than the people who plant them and longer than the buildings that they complement. Trees provide a union between the land and sky. Trees grouped together, like abiding friendships, develop character as they are touched by the group to which they belong. Those solitary in their posture, exposed to the vagaries of wind and weather, form differently from those that give and receive shelter from their woody companions.

There are twelve basic principles that should be part of every landscape design. The first and foremost principle, when considering the space in which one

lives, is *unity*. Unity pleases the eye and is the sense
of natural form. Unity harmonizes all the elements.
People carry their own definitions of unity with them.
When people sense that something is unattractive or
spoiled, they feel an internal imbalance. People
perceive instability when they lose their definition of
wholeness.

After unity come eleven other considerations:
simplicity, variety, balance, emphasis, repetition,
proportion and scale, contrast and harmony, elegance
of shape and line, form, texture, and color. *Simplicity*
eliminates the excess of details that have little to do
with sweeping composition. It is a matter of reducing
and eliminating frills. *Variety* is critical. Too little
variety, and there is monotony; too much, and
confusion reigns. A *balance* between extremes,
although always a challenge, will produce a pleasant
accord. Balance may be achieved by the distribution
of accents and masses carefully placed over the whole
scheme. There is no need to fall victim to symmetry,
the refuge for the unimaginative.

Emphasis occurs when the eye is directed to a
portion or object within the composition. It draws the
eye to a mild contrast in the overall arrangement.
Repetition gives variety its meaning. A variety of
lines, textures, colors, and forms arouses interest.
Proportion and scale creates a pleasing relationship
among the dimensions of length, breadth, and height.
It charms the eye, mind, and soul in ways we do not
understand. *Elegance of shape and line* provides lines
and curves that tantalize the senses without
interrupting them. *Form* is more attractive when it is
natural looking and graceful. *Texture* is the quality of
coarseness or the fineness of appearance. Up close,

texture is differentiated by size, surface, and spacing among the various parts of the whole. *Texture* can change with the seasons. The reflective values of the surface surroundings, as well as the quality of light and shadow, affect *color*.

A landscape should be endearing and enduring to the mind, heart, and soul. The challenge lies in avoiding monotony and chaos.

Groundwork

On Tuesday, Sally fidgeted at one of the dining tables in Windrow Garden Restaurant. There had been several days suggesting the coming warmth of spring, and Sally had chanced the wearing of lighter clothes for her function as an interviewer. Thick socks and loafers on her feet, a dark green, light woven-wool sweater, and camel slacks made her look more like a Kentucky horse breeder than the no-nonsense farm and restaurant entrepreneur she was. The workweek sounds of the kitchen had been still since Sunday.

Sally had arrived earlier in the afternoon to turn up the furnace for the interviewees and herself. There was no food in front of her unless one counted the coffeepot and cup stationed near the outer reach of her right hand. She shifted in her chair, leaned back, and glanced at the four people sitting at a larger table who were concentrating on completing the application forms and drinking the coffee she had set out for them. It had been a second small turnout of applicants in as many weeks.

The winter months had made it hard to secure a

reliable farmhand mechanic from their otherwise prudently solid commitments. Sally had originally resolved not to let her need rush her into imprudent decision making, but time was no longer on her side. Chores were going slow, or worse, and much remained undone. Machinery had to be repaired and reconditioned for spring use, and the work in the fields and orchards needed to be supervised. As hard as her staff worked, they were not accustomed to managing their tasks without coordination and direction. Sally could not be in the fields and the kitchen simultaneously. She needed to hire someone. She knew she needed a small miracle, but she didn't see any that she could readily identify sitting at the table.

She wanted Bill Cornweir to be well, but that would have required more than a miracle. Bill was still in the hospital. The doctors had confirmed a broken leg, ruptured spleen, and cracked pelvis. He was lucky to be alive. He would need months of treatment and mending before he would be able to return to the farm. Worker's Compensation still paid him some portion of his wages, but the health-care costs had mounted. If it hadn't been for his girlfriend, Sheila Ray, moving him to her home and loving ministrations, the hospital stay would have forced Sally's farm into the red ink side of the ledger. But the money was still flowing out rather than in. Cornweir would heal, but the farm and its needs went waiting. Sally knew she would have to hire someone who had applied during the last several weeks.

Sally glanced at the woman who sat among the group of men. She had not noticed her when she came in; she must have been distracted by the restaurant bookkeeping when the woman arrived. Sally noticed that the woman's black hair complemented and accentuated the overall care and confidence in the woman's presence. That presence held her. Sally's eyes then drifted to the woman's clothes, and she found herself almost chuckling as she noticed the sharp creases in the woman's shirt and blue jeans. She'd never known anyone who starched and ironed their work clothes that way. She looked beneath the table, and her eyes followed the firm muscled leg encased in the blue cloth and noticed the polished combat boots protruding from the pant legs. That was another surprise.

Sally glanced at the men and compared their worn, scuffed, and mud-covered boots. That's what Sally was used to in the farming country. Men in their cleanest dirty shirt, worn wrinkled jeans, and dirty boots. A properly disheveled lot who looked like they never went home from their tasks. The woman was a sharp but not unpleasant contrast.

Sally knew how to read the men who were applying for the temporary position. She was used to male farmhands. Their wives usually worked the orchards while the men did all the heavy, equipment-related work. It was a separation of labor she'd never questioned. Until now. She was comfortable and used to traditional farm operations and occupational preferences. A female mechanic applicant was an uncharted experience, and she did not know what to expect.

Sally was smiling at her own puzzlement when the other woman looked up, catching her eyes. The woman observed Sally with a steady, unwavering gaze. The openness of the gaze caught Sally by surprise. Amusement and a sudden coquettish flush overtook her as the woman leaned back in her chair, squared her shoulders, and fetchingly returned the smile. Butterflies launched themselves as Sally recognized a darting awareness rush from the base of her spine to the top of her head.

Under the woman's steady gaze, Sally's smile vanished in bewilderment, and Sally quickly turned her attention back to the paperwork in front of her. Unaccountably she wanted a drink, something to wet the sudden dryness of her mouth. She wanted something more than the coffee that languished in front of her.

It had been a simple friendly gesture. She assured herself there was nothing of consequence, no need to wonder at the meaning or intent behind those dark eyes. A friendly gesture of shared self-assurance, Sally rationalized. There was a position to be filled. The best person for the job would have to replace her laid-up mechanic and be straw boss to the hands. Whoever got the job, Sally silently asserted, had to be reliable and competent, and this was certainly not the time for partiality, preconceptions, or deceptive musings.

Over the course of the next two hours, Sally interviewed the prospective hired hands in the order in which they had arrived. She asked general questions, asked for accounts of previous employment, and asked the reasons for departure from the last job. Each man left with Sally's promise to contact him later with a decision, although she had not been impressed with the results of the first three interviews. She had little hope for the day and a sinking feeling about the complexity of work that she was going to be facing if she could not find a good hand. Then the last man left. As nonchalantly as possible, Sally poured herself another cup of coffee and waved the woman over to the table.

The woman approached, and Sally stretched out her hand in offer of introduction. "My name is Sally Windrow, Miss . . . Miss Jeager," Sally said as she glanced at the name on the application again.

"Jeager, just Jeager. If you don't mind. Or Nicole. Or Sergeant. Anything but Miss. I haven't been called Miss since I was eighteen. And I rarely miss a thing," Nicole said, taking Sally's offered hand firmly into her own.

"As you wish," Sally remarked as she felt the firm, callused grip and long fingers wrap around her outreached hand. The clasp lingered only a second, but Sally felt the tingling warmth long after the introduction had ended.

"Please, sit down," Sally said finally, noticing that Nicole was still standing.

"Thank you."

"I . . . uh, I see by your application that you're recently retired from the Army."

"That's right. Twenty and out," Nicole responded, trying to let her voice fill the words with nonchalance.

"I see. Well, working on a farm is a bit different from . . . from . . ." Sally faltered as she looked for the occupational title Nicole had filled in the Army. She looked down the application and found an unfamiliar title and code terms.

"Mechanic. I don't imagine mechanical work on or

off the farm is too different from what I've been doing," Nicole countered.

Sally nodded and quickly read the general application information and noted that under arrests Nicole had said none. Habit would ensure that Sally took all the applicants' information and identification to the sheriff's department for verification and assurances of no criminal records.

It wasn't that she objected to people trying to mend their ways. As far as she was concerned, everyone should get a second chance. Compassion and logic held her at that juncture. Ex-felons could mend and correct all they wanted once they were set free, but not on her property. Sally simply didn't want them on the farm, around her child, or near her cash drawers. She did not intend to falter in the requirement.

"You realize the position is temporary. My mechanic's been injured. But he'll be returning once he's mended," Sally offered.

"Ms. Windrow, it's just another job. I've got a decent pension. Better than that, I've got savings. But I'm not used to being retired. I'll use my base privileges up at Fort Leavenworth. Commissary, post exchange, that sort of thing."

"There might be better jobs in town. Like with an automobile dealership?" Sally suggested.

"Might be. But like I said, or intended to say, I'm passing through. Looking for a place to hang my hat for a bit. I'm not looking to settle or start a second career. Thought that maybe my skills and intentions to leave would fit your needs and mine."

"You think you'd be happy here?" Sally inquired.

Nicole laughed despite her intention not to. "Happiness. I didn't know that was part of the job description." She chuckled and then noticed the look of confusion on Sally's face. "No offense. In the Army they never asked if I would be happy. They did want to know I was competent, and that I am. I don't know about levels of happiness. I do know it would be a bit like coming home. I'm used to hard work. I enjoy it, and I'll give you more than a fair exchange of labor for your money," Nicole said, trying not to choke at the idea that she'd be returning to something she'd run away from.

Finding the vacancy announcement in the newspaper the previous week had given Nicole possibilities. It had given her an opportunity to stop driving, to start thinking, and to try to figure what sorts of decisions she needed to come to. After several days of thinking and talking to herself, she knew one thing for sure. She knew that not only did she not know the answers, but that she also wasn't sure what all the questions might be. The advertisement for the mechanic's job on a large farming operation with room, board, and nominal pay seemed to have been sent by the powers of the universe. It could give her time. She would be able to quit the mad dash she'd labored under when she left Fort Leonard Wood. She knew it might give her the time to begin to heal the hurt and torment of her early, unscheduled retirement.

"I see. Well, I meant that it seems to me that someone with your skills and experience would be looking for something steadier."

"Not now. Really. I don't know where I want to

go, where I want to be, or exactly what I want to do when I get there. Have you ever lost everything that you ever counted on? It seems I may have retired too soon," Nicole said, glossing over reality. "Anyway, I'm adrift in my ability to make long-term commitments. There are some things I'd like to work out. I don't imagine those wonderings or wanderings will interfere with my ability to work or my ability to hear you when you say you don't need me anymore."

"I see. You should know that although it was advertised as a mechanic's position, it's really quite a bit more than that. Cornweir, the man whose job the replacement would be taking, was much more than a mechanic for the farm. I have to tell you that I came to depend on him to do more and would expect his replacement to be able to do the same."

"I had figured on as much. I said it was like coming home. Do you want to tell me what you do expect?" Nicole asked, wondering if her interviewer was trying to discourage her from applying or beginning to make excuses for not hiring her.

"Well, for example, last year Cornweir built an addition on the lambing pens. When some of the machinery broke, he welded what needed fixing and got us back in operation. Then, because we have a lot of visitors here who pick their own fruit, it's important to keep up the appearance of the place. He hired and supervised some young men who painted the barns and several of the sheds.

"The job requires an ability to do those things plus do sheet-metal and concrete work, and have a willingness to fill in and do just about anything that needs doing. Except for the kitchen, that is. The more Cornweir did, the less I had to worry about hiring the work out to some company or group who would charge me an arm and a leg."

"I see." Nicole leaned back in her chair and thought about how best to respond to the misgivings she'd heard in the other woman's voice. "Do you think any of the other people you've interviewed would be able to do the tasks you mentioned?"

"What do you mean?"

"Let's see, you have all the applications in front of you, and you've had an opportunity to talk to each applicant. I don't know what sort of follow-up you'll do, but I don't think any of them can produce the excellent performance evaluations I can," Nicole said. She took a long sip of coffee while looking over the rim at Sally. As she watched Sally shuffle through the stack and glance at the notes she'd taken during the interviews, Nicole felt confident even if she didn't get the job. Her truck was packed. She figured she could always head west and see what retirement fishing was like.

"These men are all from around the area. Their sources would be easy to check. Most of them have worked for a number of farmers in the area . . ." Sally began by way of explanation.

"That's my point," Nicole interrupted. "That's what I heard them discussing at the table while they waited for their interviews. There is a lot of experience in the group. There was also a lot of instability, at least from my perspective. By the sounds of it, unless what you've got there shows different, most of those fellows would drop you and move on for anything that offered a dollar or two an hour more. It wouldn't matter to them whether your lead mechanic was back or not. They'd just go."

"You're a quick judge. Are you sure you're right? Or are you simply trying to use anything you can to prove your own case?" asked Sally.

"Experience. And I listen. I listen to what's said, watch people's faces while they say it, and pay attention to what their bodies do while they talk. Twenty years in the military teaches an awful lot about people. Being a quick judge of character is vital. There, it's a matter of survival. I'm not often wrong. I think they would work for you, but they certainly don't have the ability to hang in and stay here when something better might come along. I can do that. I can do the job as well as any man, better than most. For you, the combination of my abilities and willingness to be here until you say the job is done is a dual benefit."

"You think that you're the best person for the job?"

"I think for what you want — someone who's reliable until you tell them it's time to go — yes. I know what kind of work I do; my papers speak to performance and durability. What I might not be very knowledgeable about, I can find out."

"You're very sure of yourself."

"The Army never paid me to be a shrinking violet. Shyness doesn't get promoted. Reticence wouldn't have made a good temperament as a career soldier. Simple as that," Nicole asserted. She decided that if she was to lose the job she would do so on her own terms.

"I see," Sally said, wavering between an admiration for the sergeant's assertive, self-assured statements and an uncertainty as to how well she would fit into Windrow Garden and the community of people there. "Then you'd be willing to take things as they come? You'd be here, do what needs to be done, and, if it doesn't work out or when Cornweir returns, you'd have no problem with going and leaving it at that?"

"Your advertisement said you'd likely need someone until October or so. That would suit me fine. If you let me go sooner than that, fine. I'm a free agent with no other obligations than the ones you'd require if you hired me," Nicole explained.

"Sergeant, I don't hire lightly, and I don't fire lightly, either. If I hired you, you wouldn't be in the dark about what I wanted or how long you'd be staying," Sally said, ruffling at the cavalier behavior the woman seemed to expect of her.

"I have no doubt about that. By the looks of your property I figure you treat people and things with good care. I know you're trying to be careful with whom you hire. Hiring is always a risky business. But I can tell you that I'm honest, I work hard, and I won't get in your way."

"Get in my way?" wondered Sally.

"Yes, ma'am. I don't bring my personal life home. I won't be any trouble."

"Personal life?"

"No need to raise that startled eyebrow at me," Nicole said, chuckling. "Everyone has a personal life. I'm simply saying I'll keep mine to myself."

"Can you explain that . . . I mean, what do you mean?" Sally asked cautiously.

"No. However, let me assure you of a few things. I drink, but I'm not a drunk. I don't do drugs. I've never been in trouble with the law, and I won't be. I don't run with a bad crowd. And even if I did, they'd never come here. Promise."

"I see," Sally lied, trying to avoid the twinkle she noticed in Nicole's eyes. "You hinted at being familiar with farming operations?" she questioned, changing the topic.

"Yes, ma'am. When I was a kid, my folks had a dairy farm up in Michigan. We ran a little over fifty head, cultivated two hundred acres, and had the usual assortment of farm critters. It was a small farm, and we did everything the hard way — by hand with antiquated equipment. I haven't forgotten much. Couldn't if I wanted to," Nicole confessed.

"You're not going home, then?"

"I'd rather we not go there conversationally, if you don't mind. Let's leave it that there's nothing there for me. I'm sure that whatever I forgot about farming, I'll remember how to do in short time," Nicole said, unconsciously waving a hand to move the past away.

"Aren't you curious about the pay?"

"Your ad said room, board, and competitive salary. Perhaps you could tell me what that means in this part of the country and for this type of work," Nicole requested as she poured herself another cup of coffee.

"We provide housing. Whomever I hire stays rent- and utility-free. Any damage to the housing would come out of your pay. Once you start . . . well, you'd find out pretty quickly that things usually don't run nine to five on a farm. You'll be on call. Farming needs your full attention a hundred and twenty percent of the time. I figure the rent and cottage utilities to be worth about five hundred dollars a month. Most days you'll be able to eat in the restaurant if you don't cook for yourself or if you simply want to eat with the rest of us. Food's free, whether you eat it or not. Outside of that, you'll get seven hundred and fifty dollars a month . . . that's before taxes. It's the best I can do."

"Sounds fair," Nicole responded without hesitating.

"Good. That's what the men said, too. I'll be making my final decision later this week. I see by your application that I can contact you at Settlers Hotel. I'll call one way or the other. Guaranteed," Sally concluded as she stood and extended her hand to Nicole.

"Very well. It's been a pleasure, ma'am, I assure you," Nicole said as she rose to take Sally's hand in hers again. She held the hand gently in her confident grasp and incorporated a moment's eye contact with Sally before nodding her head and turning to leave.

"What will you do if I don't hire you?" Sally asked as she watched Nicole leave.

Nicole turned around slowly. "Wish you the best and not one thing less."

On Friday night, Sally dialed the number Master Sergeant Jeager had provided for her hotel. She sat at her desk in her home office and listened to the phone ring over the wires. On the third ring, as she lifted a glass of wine to her lips, she heard someone pick up the receiver at the other end.

"Hello," a sweet cheerful voice lilted back to Sally.

"Sergeant?" asked Sally uncertainly. It was not the smooth contralto she remembered from the interview.

"Oh, you must want Nicky! Just a second," the woman said as she dropped the phone.

Sally could hear the woman calling "Nicky." She heard buzzing, muffled chatter and then silence. Her mind cascaded through the reasons for the woman being in Nicole's room and just as quickly turned away from the provoking speculations.

"Yeah?" a slightly breathless, familiar voice asked.

"Sergeant?"

"Master Sergeant, retired. Who is . . . Ms. Windrow?"

"Yes, Nicole. Am I . . . am I interrupting anything, Sergeant?"

"Nicole will do, Ms. Windrow. I didn't know it was you. You caught me a little off guard."

"Is it Nicole, or did I hear that you prefer Nicky?"

"Ah, actually, I prefer Nicole. Nicky is a diminutive I gave up in my twenties," Nicole choked lightly as her young companion returned to her side. The sounds of a cooing female voice drifted over the phone.

Sally took a moment to compose herself and ignored what she thought she was hearing at the other end of the line. She wanted to try to finish the conversation she had intended before she lost her nerve and hung up. She took a deep breath and began. "I'd like to hire you if you are still interested. I'd want you to move into the spare cottage. No one's been in it for a while, so it needs cleaning up. Maybe more. We'll arrange for whatever has to be done and try to have it ready for you by the time you get here. I'd like for you to be here Sunday evening or early Monday morning. I'd like you to be available to start working on some of the machinery first thing Monday. By the way, unless something unusual comes up, everyone gets Saturday evenings through Sunday off." *Everyone but me, it seems*, Sally realized.

"I can do that."

"Good. I'll tell Jake to expect you. He'll help you get familiar with our operations. I hope we'll be able to work well together," Sally said lightly. "And, I hope that cottage will suit you."

"I'm sure it will be fine, ma'am," Nicole responded. "Thank you."

"Monday, then."

"Monday it is," Nicole said and hung up the phone.

Sally stared at the phone as she lowered it onto its cradle. She hoped that she knew what she was doing and hadn't lost her good sense. Something else was hovering near, plaguing her. A curiosity fluttered against her musings as to why her heart and mind raced at the thought of the captivating master sergeant. She did not have words for it.

Once before the question had come knocking. She had managed to push it back and move forward in her life with the more certain expectations of family and community. It had been years since she had let it rise to the level of conscious consideration. The old temptation would call, and she would toss it aside like the unwelcome, uncomfortable intruder it was. In fifteen years, the only freedom she'd allowed it was its unpredictable, ghostly throbbing against the louder protests of her safe and familiar reasoning.

Chapter 4
Homestead Arrangements

Farmers are the landscape architects of agricultural Kansas. They define and modify not only the landscape but the farm's culture. Although farming is a business, and a tough business at that, environmental amenity is not—and should not be—at odds with the working character of the land or people. What most people wish to attain is elegance, as a sense of pleasing surroundings.

The work-service area, or farmyard, is generally

separate from the house but closely linked to it. The rear of the main house and the nearby buildings form the core of the farm courtyard enclosure. An arrangement of low and tall shrubs and shade trees lessens the drift of dust, rain, and snow. The arrangement is pleasant and practical. The farmyard or work-service area needs to be large enough to allow the easy manipulation of machinery and be a safe distance between buildings for fire protection and access to adjacent fields. The area should be partially screened from public view yet easy to see from the rear of the house, particularly the kitchen.

Shade trees along the outbuildings can tie in the rooflines and provide a sense of practical symmetry to the area. Shade trees planted along the various buildings will provide protection from the vagaries of wind and weather. They can also provide areas of recreation and rest for those working on the farm. Although labor is a primary function of a farmstead, rest and leisure are not to be neglected.

Windbreaks are trees planted near and around the farmstead to reduce the destructive drift of snow. Additional benefits include cool breezes in the summer and protection from blowing dirt and dust. More important, windbreaks serve as wildlife habitats and improve the general aesthetics of the land. A well-planned and maintained windbreak can reduce energy consumption for heating and cooling buildings by twenty to thirty percent. A windbreak is not a luxury; it is a practical value for those who live and work on the farmstead. Additionally, it provides for their physical and psychological well-being.

A little imagination in the creation of a windbreak or shelterbelt should be used. Curving windbreaks, instead of squared rows of trees, can provide ground protection and a sense of space in the service area. Close-planted lines of successively shorter trees back to front that relate well with the lay of the land on the north and west in a flowing L shape provide much-needed protection from the cold winds of winter.

In summer, the best protection, and one that enhances the flow of cooling breezes, is the arrangement of deciduous trees on the southwest side of the home and along the farmstead boundaries of the service area. No planting of underbrush should be undertaken that would restrict the flow of air through the taller trees.

Windbreaks and shelterbelts on the prairie are a must. They conserve the visual and ecological balance of the land. The loss of drifting topsoil and erosion are as serious today as they were a few decades earlier in the dust bowl days. The effect of wind and rain on the unprotected land can have the same chain reaction as an avalanche. That is, it's not noticed until the results pour down on your head. A balanced concern for the practical and the pragmatic cannot be ignored without consequence.

Groundwork
County highway engineer Kenneth Rooney sat in his office waiting for his secretary to put the finishing touches on the most recent highway proposal for the state planners. He was anxious and annoyed with the increasing costs of the scheme. His

fingers drummed in irritation on the top of his desk and periodically combed through his thick blond hair.

He swiveled in his chair, looked out the window, and tried to let the morning sun cheer him. It didn't do any good. He wasn't prepared, and Donald Bradley was going to be arriving for the meeting at noon.

Rooney couldn't remember any longer how he'd let the assistant bank vice president talk him into going along with the conspiracy. Had it been the country club, the friendly rounds of golf, or the friendlier rounds of drinks? They had a lot in common, and it had started innocently enough. Their ages, love of outdoor sports, and love of money and fine women had given focus to their friendship over the last two years. But those interests did not explain how or why Bradley had got him talking about the state's interest in building a highway through the county. He shouldn't have shared that information with anyone. He certainly shouldn't have listened when Bradley started to hatch the scheme about getting rich beyond their dreams.

"Damn Bradley," he spat and then winced at the kind of hell there would be to pay if farmers got wind that their property was about to be taken under the right of eminent domain for a new four-lane express from Kansas City, Kansas, to Atchison. Of the two hundred thirty-two pieces of prime farmland, only fifty-three were in Leavenworth County. Twenty of those with the best land offered charming features, scenic hollows, and wooded bluffs. They were prime real estate and development properties. And all of them were mortgaged to the hilt at Bradley's bank.

A year into the development, Bradley had used his

money and influence, Rooney's money, and their combined leverage to buy as many portions of land sitting along the proposed highway as they could. Their resources had purchased most of the land through tax-indebted farmers and bank-forced foreclosures. They had been lucky and bought much of the land for pennies on the dollar in value.

The parcels that nestled under the new blue lines of Rooney's map would be resold to developers and franchisers as the new highway scored through the western edge of the county. But with all the wealth of possibilities before them, Bradley had insisted that they needed more. Three damned farmers stood in their way. Temple's Dairy Farm near Bashor, Gnew's Orchard near Tonganoxie, and Windrow Garden southwest of Leavenworth were yet to be approached.

"Call, you bastard," Rooney said, glaring at the phone. He'd begun to get nervous lately. All of his ready cash and liquid assets were tied into the future. He knew Bradley didn't give a damn about him, and he was beginning to feel the crunch. He glowered at the map on the wall and the orange-tinted patches indicating the farms they didn't have in their pockets yet. He knew that if those property owners caught wind of the highway, if they protested, if there was an investigation into the consortium who owned the land and right-of-way . . .

If, if, if. He could hear Bradley laughing at him now.

"If nothing. As long as you keep your mouth shut," Bradley had told him during their last meeting, "we'll own everything we want to if you don't panic."

"But what if they find out?" Rooney protested.

"No one is going to tell them. Leastwise the state. I need a little more time for the remaining farms to add to their debt. Trust me. I know how to appeal to these folks' egos. We'll have them borrowing money and stretching themselves to the breaking point. And break they will. I'll make sure of that. It's the devil in the detail and the loan contracts, if you know what I mean. They never really understand what they sign. They're always too anxious for the money. It will be my own special 'in the best interest of the bank' clause addition that will put them in our pockets. We'll foreclose, and then all I have to do is pick it up at the sale," Bradley explained. "Simple."

"Windrow is not going to do that. If she learned anything from her father, it was how not to be a fool," Rooney insisted.

"Maybe. I can be very charming and persuasive, however."

"Meaning?"

"Meaning, the lady and I are seeing each other. Meaning, you don't have to buy what you own by marriage."

"Are you going to marry her?"

"That's the plan. Although I slacked off on the courtship lately, I can pick it up quick enough. Not like there's a whole lot for her to choose from around here," Bradley said, straightening his tie in the reflection of the kitchen chrome.

"You'd do that? You'd marry someone to get her money, her property, just like that?" Rooney asked in awe of his silent business partner.

"Hell, yes. Think of it as a two-for-one deal. I get the property and the woman. She's a lonely widow and quite attractive, too. Kansas does have laws that favor my making the decisions for her when it comes to the property. She works too hard. Besides, what woman wouldn't rather be waited on? I think it's about time she took a break and learned to enjoy life," Bradley asserted.

It had been more than a month since Rooney had received those assurances from Bradley. His confidence had been bolstered by his partner's certainty, but now the plan was in its last stages of development. He would be required to submit the proposal to the state highway engineers for inclusion in the new fiscal year. Rooney wanted assurances again. The state would make the plans public once they were approved. That approval would first raise questions and then a hue and cry from every corner when it was done.

Assistant bank vice president Donald Bradley frowned and glanced at his watch. His ten-thirty appointment was late. Doug Harkner was in financial trouble again, and he was late for his ass chewing. Tardiness irritated Donald. People who didn't pay their loans on time irritated him. But people who bounced checks didn't irritate him. They pissed him off. Doug Harkner had become a constant source of irritation and a serious bad mood for Donald. With three hundred dollars of bad checks, a car loan four months overdue, and the audacity to be late for their meeting, Donald's blood pressure was rising.

Donald swiveled his high-backed chair around to look out through the wide expanse of the bank. His glass-walled office provided him with an all but complete view of the staff and tellers as they performed their tasks with customers and clients in the lobby. He liked the view. He liked being in charge of making sure others were doing what they were supposed to do. His promotions from teller up to his present position had been sure and swift because he made sure he knew what he was doing and what other people were not.

Fifteen years ago he'd arrived at the bank with the ink barely dry on his master's degree in accounting and banking. Fifteen diligent years of investing time and money, of going the distance and of keeping notes on his fellow workers had got him where he was today. Money was his life and making it was his mission, but presenting the best example of compassion was his forte. He lacked one thing, the last thing on his life's list of things to do. But he had the plan in motion. That's what counted. The regional banking president had told him what he needed to do to ensure his continued rise in the industry. It was simply a matter of getting to the bottom line.

Annoyed with the late appointment, Donald tossed the file folder with Doug Harkner's name on it across his desk and turned back to his computer screen. In his impatience he missed seeing Harkner hurry through the automatic doors of the bank.

At forty-two, Doug Harkner looked like the sum of his misfortunes and missed opportunities as he stomped past the lines of customers waiting turns in front of the tellers. Thinning dark hair waved wildly from underneath a grease-encrusted ball cap. His worn peacoat, work slacks, and unlaced construction boots bunched and bobbed as he made his way across the lobby floor.

He wasn't happy about being in the bank, and it showed on his face. He knew that Bradley would have nothing positive or hopeful to say. And he knew that he was in enough trouble to get a year in the county jail if the bank insisted on pressing charges. Doug also knew that there wasn't a damned thing he could do about it. His luck, mostly bad, had not changed over the last six months.

Doug stopped outside the clear glass door and looked in at the profile of the man sitting inside. He could see the sure, swift movement of the man's hands on the computer keyboard, the tenseness in the clean-shaven face, the chiseled jaw, and firm set of the mouth. Doug knew that Donald Bradley was not a man to trifle with in any fashion. A former college football player, Bradley had not lost the powerful build nor had he let his desk-hugging work life reduce the tone of power in his body or increase the width of his waist.

Doug screwed up his courage, placed his hand on the doorknob, and tried to remember what promises he would tell Bradley he intended to keep.

Donald Bradley heard the latch of his door click and looked up into Doug Harkner's wide, uncertain eyes. "I've been expecting you," Donald said smoothly. He would save his anger. He would let it grow as he hammered him during a recitation of his errors. Then when he had him where he wanted him, he would let him know he was going to go to jail.

"Sorry, Mister Bradley," Doug said, whipping his

cap off his head as he walked toward Bradley's desk. "That car of mine broke down again. I, it needed a battery jump. I got here quick as I could."

"Let's get to it. Sit down," Donald said as he reached for Harkner's file. He opened the file and flipped through the pages as Doug settled into the chair and waited. Donald let him wait. He made a show of pretending to read the printed information, of letting a smirk slip across his face, and of growling his discontent. He wanted Doug to squirm, wanted him to relax enough even in his squirming to consider the possibility of hope. Then he would dash it. He waited to speak until, in his peripheral vision, he saw Doug's head begin to swivel as his eyes wandered aimlessly around the room searching for something to look at.

"Mr. Harkner, it appears you're up to your neck in trouble," Donald said, letting the folder drop between his hands onto the surface of the desk. He folded his hands and waited for a response.

"I've had a run of bad luck . . . I never intended for things to get this far," Doug offered.

"Oh, so you never intended to write those checks? Someone forced you to take money from this bank?"

"It's not like that and you know it."

"Do I?"

"Of course you do. I've been a customer of this bank for twenty years. I've had some rough times, but I always recover," Doug protested.

Donald looked at the folder and placed his right hand palm down on the thick file. "Is that what you call writing bad checks? A rough time? Seems more like a tendency toward making illegal loans. You expect us to tote the brunt of this while you recover? What I'm interested in right now is just how are you going to recover from this?"

"I'm looking for work."

"That's what you said last month when we talked about the overdue note on your car," Donald asserted. "That was before you wrote these," he said as he thumbed the corners of the stapled insufficient-funds checks.

"Honest, I'm still looking for work. Things are pretty tight around here," Doug said as he tried to remember to sit up straight in his chair.

"I thought Sally Windrow hired you. Didn't you tell me that the last time we talked?"

"I thought it was a sure thing. I really did. I mean, you know her. Least that's what you told me before I went out there. Anyway, I didn't get hired."

"Why didn't she hire you?"

"I don't know. I used your name on my application like you suggested. Even told her you'd vouch for me. Doesn't seem as though you have as much pull with her as you thought." Doug chuckled in spite of his predicament. He knew that Donald fancied himself a ladies' man. He'd heard rumors that he and the Windrow woman had been seen together.

Donald frowned at the news. He'd met Sally Windrow last year when she'd come in to remortgage the farm to start the restaurant. He'd been concerned then that she might be taking on more fiscal uncertainty than she could handle. She had turned out to be a bright, good-looking woman, and he'd found it hard to refuse her. Besides, the property she'd mortgaged was worth four times what the bank had financed for her. It had been a good risk. She owned one of the most profitable pieces of property in the county. He'd spent months of time, energy, and money getting to know her better. He thought it had been paying off. Now he was not so sure.

"You mean to say she didn't hire anyone after Cornweir was injured?" Donald asked uncertainly. Not hiring a replacement for Cornweir didn't seem like a risk Sally Windrow would take. He'd assumed that with his vouching for Doug she would hire him. He'd assumed their infrequent dating would keep her interested in him while he could incidentally keep track of events on the farm. He realized he had assumed wrong. That worried him.

He made a mental note to call her and ask her out again. He was going to step up his interest in her. He had to. She had been difficult to approach, seemingly wearing her widowhood like a shield against his advancements. He had been patient, letting his practiced charm wear her down and, hopefully, win her over. He had been content not to rush or try to push the relationship. He had believed she would be ripe and willing for the picking and choosing in his own sweet time. He had plans for her, for her property, and for his pleasure.

"Well, who the hell did she hire?" Donald demanded.

"Shit, I don't know. But Charlie over at the co-op said it was some woman. Her hired man Jake Grimes was telling them all about it when he was in picking up the seed and feed for the Windrow place."

"A woman?"

"That's what I said," Doug insisted, vexed. "Tall woman, good looking too. If it's the same one, I saw her at the interview. Uppity sort."

"Who is she?"

"Hell if I know. Can you imagine that though? I mean, what farmer in their right mind would hire a woman mechanic or a woman for anything else on a farm?" Doug asked, seeing his opportunity to try to place blame for his bad luck on anything but himself.

"She hiring any extra hands?" Donald asked.

"How should I know?"

"You better make it your business to know, and I'll make it worth your while," Donald suggested. He knew that what he didn't know could hurt. He intended to use Doug to keep tabs on Sally and the workings of the farm while his other plans came to fruition. Without an informant like Doug he would have to resort to other measures. Bank loan or no, she was a prize catch. Dating her was a social coup. He couldn't afford to let her slip through his fingers now.

"Like how? I ain't no field hand. I'm a mechanic. I'm not going to work for no damned minimum wage!" Doug said, leaning closer to the desk and glancing at the glaring red ink on his overdrawn checks.

"Yes, you will, or you'll see the inside of the county jail up close and personal. It's simple. This is the time of year they do a bit of extra hiring. Part-time stuff mostly. You go back, get on, and stay on. I'll take care of these checks. If you come back with some information and maybe do a few extra little things for me if I should ask, I might see a way to get that car of yours paid off."

"Why would you do that, Mr. Bradley?" Doug inquired, wondering at the nature of the banker's sudden generosity.

"That's between me and the bank. What I want from you is to know who she hired and anything else that goes on out there. For that, and whatever else needs to be done, you'll get to stay out of jail. You only have one option: Take work out there as a field hand or cozy up to other lowlife while you serve time for bad checks."

"What if she won't hire me?" Doug stretched in panic.

"I'll work it out with her. I've got a little influence," Donald said. *But a lot less right now than I thought,* he admitted to himself. "In the meantime, and until you and I are square with your attempted defrauding of the bank, I'll keep these checks."

"That's blackmail," Doug protested.

"No, it's not. It's a choice you get to make. Having someone out there on my side is very important to me. Not being in jail sounds like it's important to you. Think of it as a contract for mutual benefit." Donald clasped his hands and waited for Doug's answer.

"I still can't live on minimum wage," Doug countered.

"You won't have to. Ms. Windrow has housing for hired hands out there. One part's set up to house temporaries. Just tell her you'll need a place to stay." Donald's mind was whirling with ideas and details.

The game plan was beginning to take on form without having to think much about it at all. He mentally kicked himself for not seeing before how much he really needed to have someone out there on the farm. He'd tended to every other detail of a new investment. Now he would ensure that nothing happened to the last piece of the puzzle. "Anything would have to be better than that shack you've been living in. They get free food out there, too, from what I understand. Hell man, you'll probably live better than you have in years," Donald encouraged.

"I don't know."

"I'll call her right now. I bet you anything that we can have you out there next week. Or would you rather I call the sheriff?" Donald asked as he reached for the phone.

Doug's eyes widened into stark white hoops as he sputtered his reply, "All right. All right. I'll do it, you son of a bitch."

"Be nice, Doug. And you better change your language for real. I hear Ms. Windrow doesn't approve of that sort of talk anywhere around her daughter," Donald said paternally as he grinned at the wilted Doug. Doug nodded in dejected acceptance as Donald dialed the phone.

"She gonna take your word just to hire me like that?"

"I think so. Particularly if you're just a temporary. If you'd read the want ads in the paper this morning, you'd know she was hiring again. But then, if you'd done that we might not have had the opportunity to be partners."

At eleven-thirty Donald could see that his day had taken on a much rosier glow. Doug Harkner was on his way to a grateful Sally Windrow who had been having difficulty finding part-time temporary help. He glanced at his watch and saw that he had plenty of time to get to his other meeting with the waiting county road engineer.

Chapter 5
Planting, Pruning, & Grafting

Tree and shrub planting. The best time to plant or graft trees is while they are still dormant. Dormancy usually occurs from late October to early April. Spring planting yields the best results and keeps the tree from suffering from winter winds or frost damage. Make sure the ground is frost free before starting.

Make sure the roots are kept moist. The planting site should be large enough to allow the roots to spread out and quickly take support in the earth. When you plant, you might want to carry a pair of sharp pruning shears to remove any damaged or excessively long, spindly roots and broken branches. Roots should never be folded to force a plant into the planting site. Such force will shock the plant and retard its growth.

Pack soil firmly about the roots to eliminate air pockets that might cause the fine root hairs to dry out. If the soil is dry, apply water immediately after planting. Build a little earthen saucer at the base of the plant to help it hold the necessary water when it is applied. Never tamp wet soil; it will cake, compress, and starve the root system. Use only slow-release fertilizers on your new plants. Don't overfertilize; it could burn the tree or cause it to grow willowy.

Pruning. The natural form of a plant is beautiful. It should be enjoyed and preserved. It is sometimes necessary, however, to help manage a plant's growth. Pruning should be done during the late winter or early spring. Pruning involves trimming unnecessary or unhealthy growth to benefit the remaining portions of the plant. Among the best reasons to prune are the following: to remove dead or injured portions; to ensure light and air in the interior growth mass of the plant; to encourage root growth and prevent dieback of branches; to rehabilitate plants that have suffered from neglect, poor growing conditions, or disease; and to stimulate the growth of larger flowers and fruit. At planting time (but not until the plant has been sufficiently established) and during the first few years, pruning is a training function to aid the plant in setting up a strong framework. Caution: Too much pruning will stunt even the hardiest tree.

Grafting. Grafting creates a successful union of two diverse but related living things in such a way that the nutrients will connect and nourish each portion. Both the stock and scion are wounded before they are matched. It is from these bound wounds that a mutual callus forms. The interweaving calluses establish the successful union of the graft.

One aim of grafting, aside from the creation of a sturdy new plant, is to assist plants in adapting to adverse climates and soils. Each benefits and each receives strength from the other. Compatibility is essential for grafting. Compatibility can be established by studying similarity in vigor and particular physiology.

Graft surfaces must hold together and be protected from trauma. There are a variety of grafting methods. Whip or tongue, splice or die, cleft and notch, wedge or bridge, are most common. Whip or tongue is used when the stocks are just about equal. Two cuts are made. The first is long and smooth, cut from below to above, and about one-and-one-half-inch in length. The scion (grafted portion) is prepared before with cuts of exactly the same size and shape. The two portions must be helped to hold together, unless there is a perfect fit. Use twine, tape, or wax to keep the graft from drying out. Tongue grafts are usually tied with adhesive tape and later removed when the new growth begins in earnest.

Other types of grafting are more complicated. Remember that grafting is somewhat traumatic. Care should be taken to nurture, treat, and maintain the grafting site. Time, patience, and sturdy bindings will heal the union and allow an alliance to emerge.

Groundwork

On Saturday morning Sally, Gwynn Marian, Jake, and Martha entered the cottage nearest the oldest hay barn for the first time since late fall. They were not surprised to see that an assortment of tiny creatures had used the cottage for a refuge from the frigid winter. Spiders and their webs, mice nests in drawers, and signs that squirrels might have invaded the attic were everywhere. Dust and an overlay of grime pervaded the cottage. They looked at the interior, looked at one another, and shrugged in mutual understanding of the task that lay ahead of them in preparing the space for livability.

"Well, I sure hope this is worth it," Martha mumbled as she stood in the short cool interior of the small living room. She was a large robust woman, and cleaning house wasn't her favorite hobby. Since she'd married Carl ten years ago, she had taken over the care of the plants in the greenhouses, the chickens, and the minor livestock. She liked that. She liked the feel of rich seedling soil in her hands, the care of the creatures' lives she managed for the farm. She didn't like doing dishes, sweeping, cleaning, or doing laundry. It had been an early complaint of Carl's. But she reminded him that he had known that when he married her. Carl adjusted. He'd become a fairly good homemaker himself. He had discovered that taking on a few of the extra chores in the house after working in the fields was easier than arguing. He never had been a disagreeable man.

Sally shouldered by Martha where she'd planted herself at the door. "You can't expect someone to come to work and have to start by cleaning out this mess, can you?" Sally headed for the small dining area and toward the tinier kitchen and the closet that held the water heater. "The sooner we get started, the sooner we'll finish," she advised. "Gwynn, honey, why don't you start vacuuming in the bedroom?"

"I'd rather be out riding," Gwynn Marian mumbled as she kicked at the ancient Hoover upright.

"We'd all rather be doing something else. But the sooner you get finished, the sooner you'll be up in the saddle. Get it?" Sally said as she raised a warning eyebrow at Gwynn.

"Slave labor," Gwynn Marian mumbled loudly as she dragged the vacuum cleaner toward the bedroom.

"That's why we have children," Martha called to Gwynn and grinned widely at the sagging shoulders of the girl as she disappeared into the bedroom.

"Don't tell her stuff like that," Sally responded, but she couldn't keep the chuckle out of her voice.

"What my mama used to tell me. You were raised here. What'd it feel like to you?"

"Well . . . still, it's not the way I want Gwynn Marian to feel," Sally asserted, remembering how she had sworn she'd never live on a farm again once she got married. *Never say never,* she reminded herself. "Let's get this show on the road."

"Couldn't start or end too soon to suit me, either.

Not soon enough," Martha sighed, resigning herself to the chores.

Jake had turned the water pipes back on and checked for leaks. At sixty-five he was still nimble, quick, and flexible. Although he would have told anyone who cared to ask he was not as quick or nimble as he once was, his energy seemed to come from his small wiry frame. Whipcord lean, most of his own teeth, and no more bad habits than he could afford, he was a vigorous, aging man, amused by what the world had taught him, and still on the alert for anything else it might have up its sleeve. He favored dark blue bib overalls, plaid shirts, and heavy work boots. The only thing that changed in his clothing for warmer months was the weight of the fabric in his shirts and an absence of a coat.

Sally fiddled with the water heater, trying to make sure it worked and wouldn't blow up. As she waited for the gas to flow into the heater, she helped Martha take down the curtains from every window in the small house, fold them, and place them in a laundry basket to take to her apartment for washing.

"Damn, it's cold in here." Martha shivered as she took a bottle of window cleaner and rags out of the box of supplies she had carried into the living room. Her full, long blond hair had been smashed down on her head with a woolen cap. A light winter jacket and insulated jeans covered her body, and her hands were protected in brown jersey gloves. Her wide face reflected the coolness of the unheated interior of the house. Martha's apple-red cheeks were joined in high color by the tilted red tip of her nose.

"I can fix that," Jake said as he strolled through the living room door carrying an armload of wood.

The elbows and knees of his clothes were dusted over with spiderwebs and dirt from under the cottage crawl space. "I thought about starting a fire when y'all came in here earlier, but I plum forgot when I started messing with that water pump." He dumped the logs in a box by the soapstone and cast-iron stove and began examining the flue. A few minutes later he'd packed the firebox and set the tented logs and tinder on fire with a wooden match.

"Water heater is working," Sally said as she came back into the living room. "Say, that looks hopeful," she cheered when she noticed the flicker of fire through the heavy glass doors of the stove.

"Does, doesn't it?" Jake said as he lit his pipe in satisfaction with his own work. "Thing is, it's pretty naked in here. This sergeant got any furniture or is she gonna sit on the floor?"

Sally looked around the room, her eyes widening in recognition. "I hadn't even thought about it. I doubt she does. Traveling usually means doing it light. Crap, what are we going to do now?"

"That's a joke, right?" Martha asked, turning from a cleaned windowpane.

"What?"

"All that stuff . . . from over in your grandparents' house. We've been using that one shed as a storage bin for all kinds of things and furniture for years. Why can't —"

"Those are my grandparents' things. Their furniture. I'm not sure if I want to do that," Sally said uncertainly.

"What harm would it do? You hired her. I mean, you trust her or not?" Jake asked.

"It's not a trust issue," Sally maintained.

"Maybe not, but surely you don't want her to spend money she might not have on furnishing this place? What harm would there be in letting her use those things?" Jake insisted.

"Well . . . I suppose they are not doing anyone any good where they are. She doesn't seem like someone who would abuse someone else's property, does she?" Sally questioned.

"She wouldn't have been able to do that to government property," Martha added.

"OK, y'all win. When Carl gets done with his chores this morning, let's see what's over there and get some of it moved in here for the sergeant. Maybe I should charge her more for her rent off her salary," Sally lightly suggested.

"Don't get stingy, Sally girl. That's not like you," Jake said objectionably.

"I'm just kidding. It's just that this is a bigger project than I'd counted on."

"As long as that's all it is," Jake cautioned.

"Mom, there's an iron bed in the bedroom. That's one thing we won't have to move," Gwynn Marian said as she pushed the vacuum cleaner into the living room.

"One less thing," Martha said, rolling her eyes to the ceiling.

"Come on, the more we jack-jaw the longer it's going to take," Jake said, stirring the fire in the stove and shutting the door.

Late Sunday night, as the hands of the old mantel clock clicked toward midnight, Sally sat in front of her fireplace mending a pair of jeans Gwynn Marian had managed to rip another hole in. She saw the headlights of a vehicle turn into the driveway. She waited for a knock on her door and was surprised when long minutes passed and nothing happened. A frown crossed her face. She knew none of the hands had left the farm earlier that evening. Sundays were a time of rest after brunch. It had been a long, work-filled week. She couldn't imagine that anyone would have had the energy to go to town looking for amusements. She knew she would have seen one of their trucks pass her window. It was awfully late for most people to come for visits. Curiosity moved her from her chair, and she walked through the kitchen and out to the enclosed back porch to see where the truck might have gone.

Looking through the windows, she could see the distant glare of the truck's headlights near the barn. Her curiosity was raised to a new level and concern. There had been a rash of thefts in the county during the last two weeks. People all along Bosman Road had lost gardening equipment, tractors, and lawn mowers to thieves. She remembered hearing that the Smiths, her nearest neighbors, had lost a small garden tractor even after they'd locked it in one of their sheds for protection. Sally's mind raced with possibilities as the lights near the barn were extinguished. She grabbed a flashlight and walked out into the night to investigate. Her nightgown fluttered in the breeze and cooled her warm skin as she walked along the gravel driveway.

Sally walked cautiously toward the outbuildings. She noted no lights in the farmhands' living quarters and wished someone was up to go with her.

Slowly, her feet muffling the crunch of gravel under her bedroom slippers, Sally walked toward the old hay barn. It rose dark and lumbering under the moon-bright night. Two stories tall, one hundred feet wide, and made of stone and lumber, it was an ancient reminder of the lost art of farm construction. Like the greenhouses, it had been designed as a practical storage structure during her grandfather's reign. It wasn't intended to be regal. Its purpose was practical and humble, but it was aristocratic compared to the steel-strutted, low-framed replacement barns in contemporary use. Only her family's continuous care and luck had made it one of the last of its kind in the county. Fire, wind, hail, lightning, and neglect had claimed all the others that had once dotted the landscape that rolled east to the Missouri River.

A high glowing light lit the winding driveway where she walked and cast her shadow out before her into the darkened distance. The moon's bright glare, weak in comparison, struggled to complement the human-made light. Sally walked toward the barn, out of the light, and into the moderate glow of the moon. She looked toward the barn, puzzling and straining to see the darkened form of the truck. She suddenly realized why she couldn't see it. It was gone. Disappeared. Her abrupt realization made the hair stand up on the back of her neck, and she hesitated with the flashlight frozen in her grasp. She was certain she should go back to the hired hand housing and get Carl or Jake.

"Aren't you the least bit chilly in that outfit?"

Sally gasped and whirled at the sound of the voice. Her arm shot up, and she snapped on the glare of the flashlight. It flew out of her frightened hand, arched high, landed hard, and rolled across the roadbed.

Nicole waited in silence as the flashlight clattered to a halt next to her booted feet. She doubted Sally knew how the light revealed her naked form through the gossamer shadow's edge of her nightgown. Nicole knew, and she silently thanked the light and the moon for their favors. She was also grateful for the shadowed darkness that covered her and the undisguised appreciation on her face.

"You startled me," Sally managed between teeth clenched in alarm.

Nicole bent down and slowly retrieved the light. Rising again, she looked at Sally and cleared her throat of the hunger that threatened to keep her speechless. "I didn't mean to frighten you. I happened to see you walking out here and, well, I know April is just around the corner, but isn't it still a bit early for moonlight walks?" Nicole asked as she walked into the circle of light where Sally stood.

"What are you doing out here?" Sally asked, trying to find her footing in the uncomfortable situation. Her initial shock and fear had disappeared the moment she realized that thieves were not accosting her.

"I work here, and I'm just settling in. I wanted to be here as you expected . . . in the morning," Nicole reminded Sally as she extended the flashlight. "Seeing you walking around out here, well, I wondered if everything was all right or if you needed anything."

"You keep late hours," Sally responded huffily as she accepted the flashlight.

"So do you, by the looks of it," Nicole responded softly, trying to keep the amusement from her voice. "I haven't had anyone give me grief about the hours I keep since I was fifteen. You weren't waiting up for me, were you?"

Sally thought she heard an insinuation in the sergeant's voice, and it fluttered against her imagination.

Without wanting to, and being unable to keep herself from it, she clasped her arms protectively around her breasts. "You're right. It is late and cool out. I'd better get back inside." Sally wavered, and then took a step backward in retreat. Halting, she heard her own voice say, "Actually, perhaps I should ask if you need help or if there is anything I could do . . ." She intended to be polite, but the words mixed the signals in her head. Her question and gestures made her falter. *The woman will think I'm crazy.*

"No, I'm unloading my stuff. No reason for you to stay out here and get chilled. By the way, I took the truck around the back of the barn to get it out of the way. It's all right if I park back there, isn't it?" Nicole asked, trying unsuccessfully to ignore her riveting awareness of Sally's pouting breasts. The image and her imagination played tag with aroused interest.

"Fine. Then you have everything you need?"

"For the time being, anyway." Nicole swallowed her complete reply. She took one last glance at Sally and the gossamer image in the halo of light before walking back into the dark.

"I'll send Jake out to you tomorrow. He'll help you get settled in and answer any questions you have. Good night," Sally offered over the expanding distance between herself and Nicole.

"Goodnight, Ms. Windrow. Sleep well."

Chapter 6
Seeds & Seedlings

The characteristics, attributes, and prototypes of seeds produced vary greatly according to diversity, variety, and environment. Some seeds are ready to germinate right after they are produced, where others need a period of dormancy, a period of cold, or fire before they will grow. Some grow swiftly while others take a long term to achieve their realization.

The way one harvests, seasons, and stores seeds depends upon the germination standards and the factors that influence dormancy of each type of seed. For example, some seeds, including many tree seeds, must never be allowed to become scorched or otherwise dry out before planting. Such seeds should be collected as soon as they are ripe and carefully rescued so they cannot become depressed and die from lack of necessary nourishment. Most other seeds, because they are hardier, may be stored in a dark dry place but may require scarring or special cold treatment before they will break their dormancy and germinate.

There are a number of reasons why seeds remain dormant. Some, such as walnut, olive, peach, plum, and many flowers and shrubs, have very hard coats or layers in which they hide to protect themselves. They must be pierced or injured before they begin to absorb the nourishment offered by water and to germinate naturally. In nature, winter heaving and weathering scarify the seeds naturally, but you must do it yourself by tapping them, filing them, or rubbing them. This process of natural or forced buffeting and touch awakens the germ to growth. If the new growth is there, then the true nature of the seed, with time, circumstance, and your careful, guided handling, will bring it to fruition.

Groundwork

Nicole woke early the next morning and cautiously poked her nose out from under the covers. The chill damp air of the morning invaded the room and caused her to shiver even as she snuggled under the mound of quilts that covered her. She groaned and rolled over to look at the radio clock. Its bright red numbers glared the time at her and warned that five o'clock was quickly approaching. Taking a preparatory deep breath, Nicole bravely flung the covers away and jumped out of bed. Her feet hit the woven, multicolored rag rug and were quickly chilled by the creeping cold from the floor underneath. She bent down, retrieved the socks she'd carelessly tossed into her boots last night, and danced from one foot to the other fighting to stay upright as she pulled her socks on. Nicole quivered at the touch of the cool room air invading the warmth of her body as she pulled on the jeans over her bare legs. As she left the bedroom, she grabbed the thick blue cotton work shirt from the hook on the door and jogged to the potbellied stove in the small living room.

Near the stove she found a bundle of old newspapers and wadded up the sports section before stuffing it into the front of the stove. She picked small bits of kindling and larger cuts of wood and lit the packed little stomach of the stove with a wooden match. "Hurry up," she commanded the tiny blue and yellow flames as they caught and crackled hopefully at her. Closing the stove door, she dashed back to the bathroom and turned on the shower for what she hoped would be a hot shower. She intended to stay in the hot water until the stove warmed the living room.

She showered and changed her clothes for more protective layerings and walked back into the living room/kitchen area. She had unpacked her automatic coffeemaker the night before and was grateful to see the hot fresh brew waiting for her.

As she sat in front of the potbellied stove, Nicole

relaxed as the fire's warmth reached out to her and began to warm the rest of the room. She tried not to look at the boxes and bags of belongings she'd brought in and left scattered on the floor from her truck. Everything would have to be put away. She would have to find order and reason in the arrangement of her life over the next few months and accustom herself to the world as a working civilian. She closed her eyes and tried not to think about the past or speculate about the future. Her hands clasped determinedly about the hot surface of the cup, and she tried to make plans about how to best proceed in her new life.

Nicole's mind slipped away from its regime of task ordering and evoked the image of Sally standing under the wide reach of the farm light. She recalled the billowing hair at her shoulders and the frail flow of the nightgown as it tried to conceal the enticing curvature of Sally's form. The image lingered, and Nicole imagined Sally moving toward her, across the shadowed roadway, and into her arms. A protracted smile spread across Nicole's lips as she let the fantasy dominate her mind.

Suddenly a loud banging at her door interrupted her morning musings. She jumped at the sound.

A plaintive voice called to her. "You deaf in there, or what?" Nicole's fantasy shattered under the onslaught.

"Just a minute," Nicole called in irritation as she rose from her chair. "Who the hell is it?"

"Jake, Jake Grimes. Saw your lights on, Sergeant, and I thought it was about time I introduced myself," the thin, aged man answered as Nicole opened the door.

"Well, Jake Grimes, it's five-thirty. Don't you think that's a bit early for a social call?" Nicole asked, looking at the seemingly frail man standing on the front stoop.

"Not round here it's not. A bit more and we'd be burning good daylight," he responded brightly.

Nicole looked at the old man and chuckled. He was wearing a pair of blue bib overalls, a flannel shirt that revealed the top button of white long johns, heavy work boots, cap, and lined butt-length denim jacket. He looked the picture of an ancient farmer heading out to hand milk the cows at the crack of dawn.

"You want a cup of coffee or are you too much in a hurry for that?" Nicole pulled the door open to show the inviting interior of the cottage.

"Can't say I'm in that much of a hurry," Jake reflected. "You got anything to go in it, Sergeant?" Jake asked, walking past Nicole as he headed toward the stove.

"Like sugar or cream? And you can call me Nicole."

"Nah, I like the sound of the word *sergeant* and, besides, you look like one. As far as that cream goes, I'll have it only if you're one of them there teetotalers. Morning's a bit nippier than any old spot of cream would solve. Thought they told me you was in the Army," Jake replied as he pulled off his coat.

"I see," Nicole said, and walked over to the kitchen cupboard to find the bottle of bourbon she'd placed among her dishes. "This more what you had in mind, Mr. Grimes?"

"And it's Jake to you, Sergeant. You can be Sergeant and I'll be just what I am, Jake. Mr.

Grimes was my father. He was a banker and all that formality and ceremony was something I never aspired to. And to answer your question, that bottle you got there . . . it would do me just fine."

"I was thinking about fixing breakfast. Are you interested, or have you eaten?" Nicole asked as she handed the bottle to Jake. She didn't offer to pour. Looking at him, she decided that he was the sort of man who liked to pour his own. She turned around and headed back to the refrigerator to give him a bit of privacy while he decided how much noncream something he wanted to put into his coffee cup.

"Old men don't eat much, Sergeant. But I reckon you don't know that. I imagine you're pretty used to hanging around with all those strapping young fellas who still haven't got their full growth on. Leastways, not until you get them in the Army for a few years. I ate a bit before I came over. So I won't be hungry much again until closer to noon. Thanks, anyway."

"Do as you wish. I think I'll fix something just the same. If you get to feeling hungry, let me know and I'll share."

"You know," Jake said, sitting down in a chair close to the fire, "you don't really need to cook here iffen you don't want to. The girl will have breakfast ready in about an hour. She gives choices, too."

"The girl?" Nicole asked.

"That'd be Sally. The girl, meaning no harm or disrespect. I've just known her for so long. Hell, I knew her when she was just a twinkle in her daddy's eye."

"You've worked for the farm a long time by the

sounds of it, Jake," Nicole said as she returned to her chair, balancing a piece of fresh toast smeared with jam.

"More than forty years. Fell into this place when I was almost a lad. Fell in love with it and stayed."

"You and your wife stay in one of the other cottages or the duplex?"

"Never married, and I live in the duplex. I fell in love with the place, the Windrows, and been happy ever since. And, as long as we're being nosy, you ever marry, Sergeant?" Jake asked as he sipped on the treated coffee.

"No, never got around to it," Nicole responded cautiously. "I did meet some people along the way I liked an awful lot."

"One of those career women, I take it?"

"You could say that. Never got to the stage with anyone where I wanted to settle down with them. Most of that's the Army's fault, or blessing. It's not a complaint. Simply the way things worked out."

"So, what brought you here?" Jake asked, tipping the bourbon toward his cup again.

"Now, Jake. It seems to me that you're the kind of fellow who probably knows everything and more about what goes on around the farm. I can't imagine 'the girl,' as you call her, would have left you out in the cold on that one," Nicole replied.

"Ah, got me there, haven't you? So, the way I hear it, you're just passing through. Here to help out a bit and then take your military retirement and the duffel bag someplace else on down the line. Kinda young to retire, aren't you?"

"I got out in the minimum. Gives me a good start on retirement. The Army and I decided we'd seen enough of each other," Nicole offered.

"Still, it's got to feel strange starting life over at your age. You being just a pup and all. Hell, Sergeant, starting over is strange at any age. Not that I'd really know. Just seems that way to me," Jake said, shifting in his chair.

"A start is a start. And speaking of starts, aren't you the one Sally said would be showing me the ropes around here?"

"That I am. No one better qualified to do it, either. Well, that's not entirely true," Jake continued, scratching his thick white hair under his cap. "Bill Cornweir . . . you might get to meet him . . . he'd generally be the fellow to show you around. He was injured. That leaves me. And I got years of information about every damned rock, fence post, and critter that ever set foot on this place."

"Well, we might as well get started," Nicole said, rising from the chair. "I have only one concern."

"What might that be?" Jake asked as he set the coffee cup on the table between the two chairs.

"I want to know if the workday actually starts this early or were you my first-morning welcoming committee?" Nicole asked. She walked to the door and turned to wait for Jake to follow her.

"Got me there, don't you?" Jake said, grinning. The grin lined and seamed his weathered face. "Truth of the matter is, not only do old men not eat much, we don't sleep much, either. I saw your light, like I said. I was up since about four this morning. I do intend to show you around, but I'll probably have to go take my catnap round noon. Don't worry, though. By the time you're finished with lunch, I'll be back to get you. I promise after this not to make you start all your days much sooner than eight."

"It's all right, actually," Nicole said gently. "I'm used to getting up early. The Army never lets you sleep too late."

"Didn't figure it did. Then . . . then you wouldn't mind me coming over once in a while and having more of this coffee with you some mornings?" Jake asked as he headed out into the light of the rising sun.

"Not a bit. As long as you don't make it every day and you never complain about my coffee."

"Not to worry on either account, Sergeant. Sides, you make a dandy cup, what with a little flavor added to it."

"Good. Now, why don't you show me how this place is laid out and tell me about the kind of things I can expect around here."

"Follow me, Sergeant. I'm going to show you one of the sweetest-run little truck-and-flower farms you've ever imagined. You might even see why I could never leave this place."

Jake and Nicole walked to the large red barn. Inside Jake gave her the quick tour of the machinery parked there. A combine, hay baler, Cat tractor, and a camouflage-painted reconditioned postal Jeep crowded the lower floor. At the back of the barn and up on the second floor, bales of hay and straw were stacked to the rafters. Jake explained to Nicole that they were standing in the barn where Bill Cornweir had his accident. He assured her that the hay stacking problems had been rectified.

"Most of the stuff here has been winterized.

Hoses drained, antifreeze put in, and just waiting for spring. You'll probably want to get around to doing that pretty soon. I figure the girl will want us to get into the fields, orchards, and timber pretty quick. If Bill were here, he'd see to it that everything was tuned and ready by the end of next week," Jake advised.

"I'll make sure it is the first thing on my list," Nicole promised.

"Now, I don't know if it should be the first thing. But tell you what, let's take a little drive and see if there are some other things you might want to do first."

Before she could ask Jake any questions about the equipment and find out if what rested before her was all there was, Jake jumped into the Jeep. As he settled behind the steering wheel he hollered for Nicole to pull open the large barn doors.

The engine roared to life under his coaxing touch, and he drove the Jeep through the doorway. Nicole shut the doors, responded to his waving, and climbed into her new transportation.

"We probably could have walked this far, but I figured as long as we were in the barn I might as well get the Jeep," Jake explained as he pulled up to two large pole barns. Nicole noticed that the barns were the same red with white that covered and trimmed the old barn. However, the sheds were different and of a more recent construction vintage. They were fairly flat on the top, and the sides were made of a sturdy-looking metal. Large double sliding doors closed over the openings. The buildings were huge, probably seventy-five by a hundred feet each. Looking at the buildings, Nicole realized that much more of the farm's machinery had to be hiding inside.

"More than likely you'll be spending a lot of time here," Jake said as he opened the driver's door and fairly jumped out of the Jeep. His spry and agile movements surprised Nicole, and she reminded herself that she shouldn't let looks deceive her. She followed him into the closest shed.

"We got standard ton-and-a-half trucks, smaller John Deere tractors with lifts, eight-ton grain-type trucks, row listers, cultivators, plows, a couple of old elevator potato diggers, a handful of fruit planters and general purpose planters, mowers, brush hogs, and more general maintenance equipment than you can shake a stick at," Jake recited as they walked through the first shed.

"There is a lot more equipment than I had figured to find on the farm," Nicole said in amazement.

"Listen, some of this stuff is older than I am and was used by the girl's grandfather. But it all works, it all runs, and we use every bit of it to keep this place green and growing. First rule of farming is, Throw nothing away. Every piece of equipment we maintain and save means a piece of equipment we don't have to buy."

"I understand that. The philosophy is a bit different from that of the Army, but I'm sure I'll be able to manage. What's that door back there?" Nicole asked, pointing to the end of the shed.

"That, Sergeant, is the door that leads to the toolroom. Your home away from home."

"Let's take a look," Nicole urged.

Nicole walked to the end of the shed and opened

the door. The room turned out to be the size of a small barn. Inside, neatly stacked, stored, and hanging on pegs or labeled in drawers and boxes were row after row of tools. It looked like every conceivable tool for woodworking, painting, leather crafting, metalworking, engine repair, welding, plumbing, and electrical might reside in the structure.

"Good grief," Nicole breathed. "This place looks like a hardware store and mechanic's dream rolled into one.

"Kinda impressive, isn't it?"

"It looks like this place has taken the idea of being self-sufficient to new heights," Nicole said as she looked around the shed. She hadn't counted on the magnitude of equipment or tools available. She'd been thinking about her father and mother's farm. There was no comparison.

"I'm beginning to see that there's a lot more to this operation than I first suspected," Nicole admitted to Jake.

"Kinda surprised you, didn't we? There're two sections to the place. That's a big chunk of land to manage. We're the biggest truck farm in this part of the state. Got the best soil for it, too. A couple of months here and we'll make a new woman of you." Jake laughed at the expression on Nicole's face.

"I'm not sure I'd appreciate that. But I can tell you this . . . The next time I roll into a town and look for work, I'm going to ask a lot more questions. Seriously, though, I think this will be just fine. I was wondering how I was going to spend my time, and now I can see I should have been wondering if I was ever going to get any time off."

"You'll have some of that. Don't worry. We might

work you a bit hard, and you might not feel like gallivanting around the country until you get used to this. But it's a good life, and you might even come to enjoy it," Jake suggested.

"That remains to be seen. So, let's go see the rest of the place. I'd like to take in the size and complexity of the operation, too. I want to understand what's done here, why and where. It will give me a perspective. I like perspective."

"All right, let's get going," Jake said as he turned to leave the shed. He beamed at Nicole and looked like a man who took his work seriously but intended to enjoy it just the same.

Over the next two hours Jake and Nicole drove through the six hundred twenty acres of the farm. Nicole watched as fields passed along the sides of the Jeep. The fields were rich — damp and waiting for spring with its revival of planting. At the far northeast corner of the farm Jake proudly showed Nicole the expanses of walnut and pecan trees crowded into a flowing, fifteen-acre cluster next to acres of blueberry, raspberry, and gooseberry bushes and apple, peach, plum, cherry, and pear trees. The need for well-maintained equipment and tools became immediately apparent to her. It was an expansive and informative driving tour.

On the drive back to the barns Nicole noticed wide sets of contoured hills with hints of buddings on the vines. She asked Jake about them. He explained that she was looking at the strawberry patches where high school students and local women would come in the late spring to begin picking the crop. The berries would be offered for sale in the greenhouses and for sale to the grocery stores in the region.

Nicole felt awe at the massive farming enterprise. Acres of vegetables were yet to be planted, a bit of wheat, rye, sweet corn, sunflowers, and the year-round offerings of the greenhouse filled her with an understanding of the obvious pleasure he took in showing her "the girl's farm." She couldn't imagine how Sally or anyone else on the farm ever had a chance to do anything other than work. She was lost in her own thoughts as he pulled the Jeep up to the barn.

"You getting hungry?" Jake asked.

"What did you say?" Nicole responded, shaking her head. She'd been trying to sort out her amazement and concern about how the workload she would be attempting to maintain until October.

"Well, you just had one piece of dry toast some two or three hours ago. I was wondering if you were still in the mood for some breakfast. I expect that Sally's up and that she might have something for you. That is, if you're interested," Jake explained.

"I didn't think the restaurant was open until Wednesday."

"Oh, it's not open for business, but Sally and Carl Marmer's wife, Martha, generally fix food for all the hired hands anyway. Didn't Sally tell you? That's part of the benefit of living here. We get to eat free and regular."

"I think I remember her mentioning something about that," Nicole replied. She couldn't imagine Sally in an apron. The image of her in the thin nightgown flashed before her eyes and impeded her view. She shook her head and thought she would wait before sitting down with the other hands for lunch. She had everything she needed in the cottage.

"Well, come on, then. Let's go see the boss lady," Jake urged as he jumped out of the Jeep and headed for the restaurant.

"No, Jake," Nicole hesitated. "I've got a lot more unpacking to do. If I don't get started now, I won't get it done."

"Have it your own way. You don't know what you're missin'," Jake chastised as he headed toward the restaurant.

"Probably not," Nicole agreed.

Sally stood at the back door of the restaurant, hidden by the shadow under the eave, and watched the exchange between Nicole and Jake. She was surprised when she saw Jake turn and walk alone toward the restaurant. Sally wondered at Nicole's shrug of the shoulders, and she was puzzled when Nicole walked briskly back to her cottage. She watched the easy, strong motion of the woman's body and the sureness of her step. Unbidden emotions played at the corners of her mind.

Sally waited at the back door for Jake and opened it for him as he came up the steps. She smiled at him as he walked into the dining area.

"If you're hungry, Jake, I think you'll like what we've got today," Sally said as cheerfully as she could manage.

"Wouldn't imagine it being any other way," he responded and watched Sally's eyes wander past him and out toward the barn. " 'Spect she's the loner type. Might need some settin' in first. Don't you worry none, though. I think I can manage to eat what extra vittles you got."

"I'm sure you would," Sally said, humoring him. She closed the back door and reached round her waist to tighten her apron strings.

"Bit tight lipped."

Sally barely heard Jake's voice through the feeling of consternation that tingled at the back of her mind at Nicole's reluctance to join the farm crew for lunch. "Beg pardon?"

"She's a bit tight lipped. It'll take a piece of time to get a real feel for her. Seen her type before. Nothin' wrong with it, but they're a little tough on the company they keep," Jake said, half to himself and half to Sally.

"As long as she can do the work, she can be as quiet and alone as she wants," Sally asserted in annoyance.

Jake looked at Sally and was surprised at the tone in her voice. "Patience, girl. I don't think you mean that. Lady's made a big change in her life. I imagine she's still sorting it out. 'Sides, woman like that can pretty much take care of herself. No need for you concerning yourself as to whether or not your new hired hand will like your cooking!"

"You sound like Dad," Sally said, smiling at Jake as she followed him into the dining room.

"Wasn't meant to," Jake said, flushing in delight. "But now you mention it, he was a pretty smart man, too." Jake chuckled and hurried into the dining room.

* * * * *

Jake filled up his plate for the second time and returned to his table. "Had to have another piece of pie. That Sally sure does good by pie."

"Sure does," Doug Harkner agreed, scooping a mouthful of cherries and crust into his waiting mouth.

Chapter 7
Cultivation & Care

Whether you have a large garden or small, one of the earliest gardening treats you may enjoy is the sweet, plump lusciousness of strawberries. The beauty of strawberries is that they may be grown indoors or out. The dark green foliage, contrasted with its early tiny white flowers and later bright red fruits, ensures a colorful addition to home, patio, or garden. Although strawberries are easy to grow, your success will depend on careful attention to cultivation needs and requirements.

Strawberries are a matter of less being more; that is, a well cared for small planting will produce more fruit than a large planting that receives less attention. If you follow good growing practices, each foot of row or container can produce nearly a quart of berries—a real taste treat and a real satisfaction.

Select a sunny, well-drained location. Wet soils reduce plant growth and increase the possibility of mold with a higher incidence of disease. Strawberries grow best in loamy or sandy soil that has been worked to a fine, mellow condition just before the plants are set out. Prepare the soil with rich natural fertilizer and other nutrients for the best results.

Mid-March to early April is the best time to plant strawberries in Kansas. However, permanently mulched beds with plants protected or indoor gardens may be established earlier to provide fresh results as early as late May. The preferred varieties, and the hardiest ones for Kansas, are Atlas, Earligrow, and Surecrop.

Be sure to use young plants with vigorous roots. Remove any damaged or diseased leaves before setting out. Dig a hole for each mother plant that is large enough to hold the roots without crowding. Mound the soil in the center of the hole and set the plant on the mound with the roots pressed firmly into the soil and around the base of the mound. Fill the hole halfway with soil, water to wash the soil around the roots, and then fill the rest of the hole with dirt. Firm the soil around the plant. Position the plant so that soil covers all of the roots but does not cover the small leaves that are developing into the crown of the plant.

Protect young plants with a cover to reduce exposure to too much sun or drying winds. Shade the young plants to keep soil moist for several days after planting to establish the roots.

The original mother plant will send out shoots of daughter runners. Though the runners appear to sit on top of the mulchin permanent mulched beds, they will send roots down through the soil and establish themselves in time. Mulch will decompose during the summer and sink, allowing the newly rooted plants to be only slightly above the soil level. This is as it should be; in time, the roots will sink deep and establish themselves for your future harvest.

Harvest of the established beds may begin as early as late May and continue through August, although typically the hot days of late summer may reduce the quality and quantity of fruit. At final harvest, you may want to thin the rows to assist the start of new runners. You may also want to provide the bed with supporting materials. The best supporting materials would be well-rotted manure, compost, and enriched leaf mold worked into the top layer of the soil. If you do this, remember to smooth the soil out again and place a six-inch mulch around the plants that have or will have a new batch of daughter runners. These runners will be next year's supply of bearing plants.

By careful selection of the best bearers, a strawberry patch may be made to produce a larger crop with each succeeding year. The heavy mulching of summer will preserve soil moisture for the young plants during long dry days, while the decomposing layer on top of the bed enriches the gradually blacker, mellowing soil below.

Fresh strawberries are a great reward for your care and commitment. Fresh berries are just the beginning, as you may find additional delights with jams, jellies, syrups, pies, and wine, depending on your tastes. Only your imagination and minor labor limit these additional delights.

Groundwork

Sally's mother, Gwynn, knew what being alone was like. Her husband of thirty-five years had died of a heart attack late one evening eight years ago. She had been at the house, cooking supper and waiting for the sounds of the John Deere tractor to chug through the farmstead and up to the barn. At six o'clock she had begun to worry. By six-thirty she went looking for her husband. It was a long walk across the fields.

She saw the tractor first. It was parked near a large oak tree that had been partially ravaged by lightning years before. The engine of the tractor was still running, churning away in the low thrum-drum of neutral. The sight of it made her wonder what her husband was up to, and she searched the wooden fence line to see where he was and why he had left the tractor unattended.

Then she saw him. He was sitting under the remaining branches of the old oak tree, and his back leaned awkwardly against the trunk. She waved to him, but he did not respond. It was as though he were in deep contemplation. Then she noticed the slouch in his body and the uncomfortable angle of his leaning body, and fear touched her heart. She ran to him on uncertain legs and knew he was dead before she fell down to hold him for the last time.

She stayed with him under the tree, pleading to him and to any angel that might listen while the sounds of the tractor and the evening breezes accompanied the soft sounds of her sobbing.

For five long years she had managed the farm with the help of the hired hands, but although the work provided comfort, it no longer gave joy. Then when her daughter had returned to the farm, a breath of fresh beginnings had seemed to sweep through Gwynn. She had decided, at her daughter's urging, to take up residence in town, snowbird to Arizona, and recreate her life.

During the first week of May of every year, Gwynn O'Conners returned to the farm to run the greenhouse sales. She could bear to return to the farm and enjoy it with her daughter and granddaughter. It was a time she looked forward to, although she did not mind retirement. Wintering in Arizona was fine, but there were only so many clubs to join, bridge games to play, and concerts to attend.

Being a widow and a woman of leisure occasionally made her feel that she had too much time on her hands. Working at the farm again gave her a break from some of her more ardent gentleman pursuers. She was grateful for the break and felt useful, wanted, and needed by her little family.

She had considered remarrying, but at sixty-one she didn't see any need to rush romance. Besides, remarrying was for Gwynn a matter of finding the right man who would let her go her own way, who would also enjoy traveling and being together, and who was a good companion. There were few who could or would meet those criteria. There was time enough for all that. Spring brought about the need to make her renewed contributions to the farm she handed over to her daughter. For the time, being at Windrow Garden again was enough. She enjoyed the farm and her necessary part in it.

Advising local gardeners about the flowers, herbs, vegetables, and fruit trees they purchased from Windrow Garden gave her a sense of daily renewal and joy. The spring and long summer months would give her time with her daughter and granddaughter and the opportunity to renew old friendships with families in the outlying county.

She loved and worried about her daughter and granddaughter. More particularly, she worried about Sally. Gwynn worried that Sally was working too hard and trying to do too much on her own. She worried that her daughter was trying to be everything to everyone as she took on the burden of running Windrow Garden and raising her daughter alone. Gwynn would have preferred for her daughter to be happy, secure, and loved. However, the way things were going, it seemed to Gwynn that Sally was getting few rewards from her hard work. Gwynn wanted Sally to love and be loved as wholly and completely as she herself had been for the thirty-five years with Sally's father. She worried that Sally might let all her opportunities for happiness pass her by.

In the greenhouse, as Gwynn put the starter change and bills into the cash register, she decided that there had to be something she could do to encourage her daughter's happiness. She determined to figure out how she could help her daughter find fulfillment.

The morning hours flew by as customers picked over the flowers and tender young vegetable plants. Gwynn took time to help each new gardener and shared tales of gardening secrets and mishaps with old friends.

Spring was the hopeful and energetic time of the year. Practiced gardeners had all but forgotten their good intentions about not wanting to overplant, and they behaved like eager children as they loaded their cars with more potential produce than they and their families could use. Novice gardeners, eyes bright with expectation and the thrill of a new hobby, came in and generally required at least one of everything. Everyone went away intent, content, and alive with the prospect of rewards for their tender purchases. Gwynn was pleased. The cash register rang its merry tune, making Gwynn wonder if the whole county was under some spell of gardening fever.

In the late afternoon, Gwynn noticed that the drip and mist lines in the greenhouse did not come on as scheduled. She walked toward the pumping machinery at the back of the greenhouse and listened to the angry humming in the pumps as they protested with the timer. A wisp of smoke seeped out of the pump housing, and the smell of hot metal wafted toward her nose. She quickly hit the emergency off switch and hurried to the phone next to the register.

She was waiting on another customer who had stacked several cartons of tiny green geraniums on the wide countertop table when she looked up to see an attractive, tall, olive-skinned woman walk in carrying a toolbox. As their eyes met, Gwynn noticed the polite whisper of a smile fleet across the woman's face as she walked to where Gwynn and the customer stood. Gwynn tried to place the woman's face and then realized that the woman carrying the red toolbox was the person Sally had hired as the farm's new mechanic.

"Are you here about the pumps?" Gwynn asked, taking new measure of the woman.

"Yes, ma'am. Could you point me in their direction?" Nicole asked, looking around the greenhouse expectantly. Her gaze came back to Gwynn when the older woman did not immediately respond. Nicole noticed a small hint of a downward turn in the older woman's mouth as her eyes flicked over Nicole in concern.

"Ma'am?" Nicole queried.

"My daughter hired you," Gwynn stated distractedly. Nicole reminded Gwynn of someone, another friend of Sally's, a friend from long ago. There was something about the woman, and the feeling coursed like a disquieting shadow through Gwynn's mind.

"Yes, ma'am," Nicole said, taking a step forward and offering her hand. "Name's Nicole."

Gwynn looked at the hand, its long fingers, strong broad palm, and accompanying calluses as she tentatively extended her own hand. She received a firm but calculated handshake. Not too soft, but warm and assured. Gwynn recognized the handshake of a person who was conscious that she could crush frail fingers of someone who might be prone to arthritis. She appreciated the mild yet full grip and preferred it to the soft lazy handshakes she'd run into before. A tiny spark of gratitude and admiration threaded through her mind. Then it, too, caught on the elusive memory from the earlier moment.

"Could you show me the pump?" Nicole asked again.

"Certainly. Funny, you remind me of someone. Or, at least I think you do. Can't rightly put my finger on it," Gwynn said, waving Nicole to follow her. "Probably a figment of my imagination anyway. Don't mind me. I've met so many people over the years that just about everyone begins to remind me of someone or something else." Gwynn shrugged as she led the way back to the silent pump and pointed to it.

"Ever have anything like this happen before?" Nicole asked as she set the toolbox down and squatted next to the pump housing.

"Can't remember, but the pump's probably older than you are. It runs the well water up through that casement attached to the rear. 'Bout all I know is that it can be cantankerous if it wants to be. 'Fraid I can't be much more help than that," Gwynn worried. The pump was essential to the heat and moisture maintenance in the greenhouse. The seedlings and tender plants could not afford to be without its necessary luxury for long. If the plants were going to survive and be sold, the misting waters and moist, heated air were absolutely vital.

"That's all right. I'll take a look at it and see if I can't convince it to get back to work," Nicole responded as she began loosening the screws on the housing.

Gwynn watched the sure quick movements of the mechanic at her task. There was no hesitation. Nicole's poised, confident response to each aspect of the job as she worked her way into the interior of the housing and the rear of the motor confirmed Gwynn's confidence in her daughter's decision to hire the woman. Not that she had doubts about her daughter's judgment, but it was nice to have her faith in Sally reaffirmed.

The tinkling of the greenhouse doorbell alerted Gwynn. "I've got to get back up front," she said, turning to leave.

"That's fine. I've got everything here I need . . . I hope," Nicole responded as she concentrated on her task.

Thirty minutes later, as Gwynn helped an elderly neighbor load her car with two boxes of Suregrow strawberries, she glanced up to see Sally walking across the roadway. As the customer drove away, Gwynn and Sally walked back to the greenhouse together.

"Nicole get here?" Sally asked.

"Some time back. She certainly didn't waste any time getting here and getting started. She seems to know what she is doing," Gwynn commented.

"Yes, Mom, she knows." Sally knew how her mother worried about the farm, and she wanted her to know that she was confident in the people she hired. Years of love and habit told Sally that her mother's offhand comments hid tiny concerns. "Is it me you wondered about because I hired a woman or were you wondering about anything else?'

"Neither. I'd probably worry for no reason about any new hand who got hired."

"Of course you would," Sally said, putting her arm around her mother as they walked through the greenhouse door. "So put your worry away and sell lots of stuff. I'm going back to see how she's doing."

"Fine," Gwynn said as she returned to her cash register to sort the checks from the drawer along with all the bills over twenty and place them in the floor safe.

Sally walked back to the pump area and found Nicole sitting cross-legged on the floor, a few parts of the pump housing spread out in front of her, and a yellow cylinder in her hand. Sally smiled to herself as she watched Nicole's eyes squint in deep deliberation as she examined the cylinder.

"Expecting it to tell you what's wrong with it?" Sally asked as she sat down on the floor next to Nicole.

"Ah, you startled me. I didn't hear you sneak up on me. Are you here to check on me and see if I can figure out the mysteries of deep-well pumps gone bad?" Nicole asked as she masked the jolt of electricity she received from the charged cylinder.

"I seem to keep surprising you," Sally proposed.

"You do that, all right," Nicole said, smiling, not sure if they were still talking about her visit to the greenhouse and the condition of the pump, or something else.

"Good," Sally said as she leaned closer to Nicole's shoulder. "I've been thinking we should be friends," Sally whispered softly.

"You have?"

"Of course. After all, we live in the same place, eat in the same place, work and sleep in the same place. There's no reason not to be friends," Sally said, justifying her decision and leaning into Nicole's strong arm for emphasis.

"So proximity and familiarity are the basis for this friendship?" Nicole breathed her quiet question and dared look into Sally's wide green eyes.

Sally diverted her glance from the question momentarily, then returned her scrutiny and searched for understanding in the dark brown depths of Nicole's gaze. "It's certainly not a bad reason. Having things in common is usually the basis of friendship, isn't it?" Sally defended. She did not know what to make of the question Nicole had asked. She didn't know if she wanted to follow the hints that she thought she heard there. The question made it seem as though Nicole was wary or doubtful, as though Sally were putting a burden on her. Sally felt the question in Nicole's eyes carry a sting of mild rebuff.

Nicole let a noiseless, distressed chuckle escape her mouth as she looked at the perplexity on Sally's face. "Ms. Windrow, we can be friends. We can even be friends on your terms," Nicole said as she touched Sally's knee lightly where it rested next to her own hip. She watched Sally's complexion sharply change tint from its normal peaches and cream to a high ruddy hue. Nicole let her fingers glide softly, and then she quickly moved her hand away.

"But I'm fairly certain we cannot be friends for

the sake of your inquisitiveness. I do not want to be run out of town or shot by a jealous boyfriend for contributing to the satisfaction of your curiosity."

Gwynn O'Conners stood rooted to a spot in the greenhouse twenty feet away from where Nicole and her daughter sat with their heads together talking. She had almost called to them as she walked in their direction. She almost spoke out to tell them how conspiratorial they looked sitting together on the floor. Then she had hesitated. Recognition had halted her and welded her where she stood. Her throat constricted at the flood of memories about her daughter and another special friend from high school. Memory came flooding back.

Nicole didn't look anything like Julie Macer. Julie and Sally had both been seventeen then. Julie was thin as a rail with short thick blond hair and an energy level the envy of her track mates. Gwynn's husband had mentioned something about Julie's behavior being a bit masculine, but initially Gwynn had laughed and ignored him. Gwynn had figured that all young women athletes, born in the spirit of competition, would garner that sort of response from a man. Gwynn had assured her husband that it was nothing to be concerned about. The girls were dating boys in their class, and she scolded him for being unkind about the girl's demeanor. She had reminded her husband that it was safer for girls not to be too wrapped up in boys at their age. There was time for all of that later. She had assured him they would marry and settle down like everyone else. Their friendship was healthy. It was supposed to be a phase in their life. It would pass, she had reasoned. Then it did not pass.

Sally and Julie had become fast friends as they discovered their love for volleyball. They became inseparable. Sleepovers, trips to volleyball camps, and spending time with each other had been something both families easily accepted until the night of Sally's eighteenth birthday. Gwynn hadn't knocked; she couldn't remember why. She'd never barged into Sally's room before. But that night she had violated a trust and found Sally and Julie wrapped in each other's arms.

A terrible, tearful row ensued. Ultimately, Julie was sent away by her parents to live with an aunt on the East Coast. Sally had been inconsolable. Time passed, and things had appeared to return to normal. Julie's name was never mentioned again, and years later Sally had married. Gwynn had forgotten Julie, the situation, the circumstances, and the concerns. Until today.

The sting of memory vaulted up Gwynn's legs and spread alarm through her soul. Her daughter stirred to rise from where she sat next to Nicole, and Gwynn fled before her daughter found her standing behind them. She ran to the far end of the greenhouse as quickly and quietly as she could. She needed, wanted, time to think, a space to be alone and to decide what she had to do to keep her daughter safe from harm.

She was standing at the cash register when Sally walked past her. Gwynn saw her daughter hesitate at the door as if there was something she wanted to do but couldn't remember what it was.

"Are you all right, dear?" Gwynn asked solicitously.

"Yes. No. I don't know, Mom," Sally responded as she opened the door to go out. She halted and let her head drop wearily on the glass door. "Do you ever find it hard to figure out what will make you happy? Is there a time or age where the answers become crystal clear?" Sally asked. Her eyes showed hints of brimming tears. "Or do we just stumble around lost and alone until we die?"

Sally flung open the door and dashed across the yard to her house.

Chapter 8
Reservoirs

There are practical considerations for having and maintaining reservoirs and ponds on a farmstead. Although they can cost you upwards of a few hundred dollars, the returns are plentiful. The benefit in fish crops, fire and drought insurance, and a stable water table are notable. The fun and relaxation of mind, body, and spirit are less reducible to dollars but are not to be ignored.

The average farm pond is a half to three acres in

size. When creating a pond or reservoir, expert help is advised. There are a large number of considerations such as rainfall, seepage, silting, fertilizer, grasses, algae, and plankton.

The pond will need to be fed by an appropriate and abundant watershed. By way of example, ten acres of pasture or woodland are needed to feed runoff water into a pond that you intend to maintain at a one-acre size at an eight-foot depth. You can starve a pond and the life in and around it if there is not proper or abundant nourishment. Worse, a shallow pond or reservoir breeds mosquitoes and can be rapidly overgrown with weeds. You will need to build a broad, well-sodded spillway. A vertical drainage pipe with its open end six inches below the level of the spillway and connected to a pipe through the dam will provide proper overflow.

You will need to protect your pond or reservoir from the unwanted intrusion of cattle or other large farm stock. They can and will break down the banks, soil the water, and create havoc with a stocked fishpond. A multiflora rose hedge makes an attractive barrier for cattle and provides a refuge for wildfowl.

For fun and pleasure, you should try to create the best possible conditions for wildlife. Natural fertilizers around the dam area will maintain the flora. It would be advisable to plant grasses and a legume-like tall sericea lespedeza, which will provide food and cover for birds and small game.

Farm ponds stocked with fish should be fished often. You cannot overfish a farm pond. Incidentally, frequent fishing will actually help to produce of more fish in the pond. The activity of unhurried fishing under the spreading shade of trees, the wisp of grasses in the breeze, the natural flora aroma on the air, and the tranquillity at the end of a hard day's work are just a few of the unsung benefits for the homestead.

Groundwork

In April the work on the truck farm began in earnest with the planting of crops and new berry bushes. Seedlings from the greenhouses, hotbeds, and cold frames were set into the soil. Radishes, turnips, spinach, kale, potatoes, asparagus, rhubarb, cabbage, broccoli, onions, shallots, and garlic were placed in the readied and conditioned acres north of the farmstead. The fields fairly hummed with the activity of planting and sowing of the first crops that would go to market in the Kansas City, Missouri, farmer's market in the River Quay area. They would be the first to bring what Sally hoped would be profit in the new year.

The second setting would produce lettuces, mustard, cauliflower, beets, basil, Swiss chard, carrots, peas, parsley, parsnip, and chicory for the forty-acre spread immediately west of the homestead. Warm-season crops of peppers, hot peppers, cucumbers, cantaloupe, pumpkin, watermelon, sweet potatoes, and small squashes would be planted in the fields that had been allowed to remain untilled the year before.

The third and last set of twenty acres would produce specialty items Sally had started in the greenhouses. Sally intended to provide herbal recipes and sample techniques to help city dwellers cope with their hectic lives. Chives, chamomile, cilantro, epazote, fennel, dill, borage, anise hyssop, sage, marjoram, balm, lavender, sorrel, perilla, thyme, tarragon, rosemary, summer savory, and ginger to make oils, vinegars, and teas for enthusiasts. It was a new enterprise and one that Sally hoped would become profitable.

Nicole was equally caught up in the swirl of activity going on around her. She worked furiously to maintain and ready the seed drills, tractors, mowers, planters, cultivators, wagons, and manure loaders. At the end of each day her back, hands, and muscles along her shoulders gave notice to the effort and strain the workload had placed on her. She began to have intimate knowledge of and a new understanding for the term *handywoman*. She was in charge of repairing fence line, forming and pouring a new sidewalk from the produce shop to the greenhouse, and welding broken machine parts and working with hot and cold metal to improvise parts for the essential machinery.

New calves, lambs, and chicks scurried in their respective pens, bleating and calling for their mothers' attentions. The earth had been turned, raked, and drilled with what seemed to be every imaginable plant and seed on earth. The fresh clean sweet air flowed through the farmstead and invigorated even the weariest worker. The sweep of aromas and smells that heralded spring, new growth, and the renewal of life overtook every activity. All able hands were turned to the work of bringing something new and tender into the world. Days started early and ended late. Nicole ate breakfast in her cottage, packed lunches for herself, and sometimes found the energy to fix supper at the end of the long days.

Occasionally Nicole would see a slick, black Le Sabre pull up in front of Sally's house and a well-dressed man emerge and go to the door. On those evenings, her curiosity overwhelmed, Nicole would watch as the man and Sally emerged from the house. Once a week like clockwork he would arrive and take Sally somewhere — perhaps into the city for dinner and dancing. Nicole never knew when they came back. It seemed none of her business. She took her body and intents into Kansas City. In the city she found everything she needed except a place to put her heart. She tried not to be interested in or concerned with any life but her own on the farmstead. The intent seemed to be working.

As the warming days of April wore on and the activity of work, repairs, and planting consumed all hands, Nicole worked alongside Jake and Carl. She worked to ensure that they had the machinery they needed and were not drawn from the fields to make minor electrical or plumbing repairs. Occasionally Jake would seek Nicole out in the early morning for a quick cup of coffee before the day began its flurry of activity. He would gently tease her about her solitary habits and bring her a few temptations from the kitchen. He'd tell her Sally had prepared the treats with her own hands.

In the third week of April Nicole noticed that Sally began to make a point of seeking her out. Nicole would be working on a piece of equipment or attempting to plan a day of mowing the underbrush near the tree line, and suddenly Sally would appear.

She would stand and wait until Nicole noticed her waiting patiently nearby. Or, if Nicole appeared to look up from her work, Sally would wave and walk to the place Nicole had stopped the machinery. She would approach smiling, while Nicole watched the tantalizing saunter. During those breaks from work, Sally would keep the alluring smile on her lips and ask Nicole how things were going and what she was doing to or with a particular piece of machinery. She would tarry and talk to her about some obscure aspect of the farming operations or make some pleasantry about the weather. Although the interruptions would give Nicole an excuse to stop work and listen in polite curiosity to her boss's inquiries, questions tugged at the back of her mind.

When the weather began its slow warming trend, Sally began to appear in Nicole's workshop, a cup of hot chocolate or coffee in her hand and an offer of conversation on her lips. The slow dance of attention and enticement jangled Nicole's nerves. Ever cautious and a little disturbed at her own intensifying interest, Nicole tried to distance herself from any desire to have more than conversation with Sally. She deliberately busied herself by going to town for parts and equipment and taking increasingly frequent forays into the city. She sought company and solace in the arms of passionate strangers, which wasn't what she wanted but seemed the best and wisest alternative. But there were frequent uncomfortable experiences when she imagined seeing Sally's face and feeling the touch of her skin while in someone else's arms.

Nicole would remind herself that Sally was

straight and that straight women were occasionally flirtatious without intending to be.

In the weeks since she'd eschewed Sally's speculative advance, what had seemed like an honorable act now weighed on her like a sin. Nicole was angry at herself and angrier with Sally for tempting her interest, initiating an absorption in dreams of palatable delights she labored busily to ignore. Kansas City was no longer succor for her turbulent libido. Sally had seen to that. Nicole had become haunted and no touch but Sally's could warm her.

The farm's atmosphere turned heavy. Like an electric storm, something threatened to crest the far horizon and vent itself across unprotected terrain.

On a Tuesday in the warming middle of May, Nicole worked through the noon hour, skipping lunch and vowing not to stop until she'd worked enough to tire her beyond any possibility of daydreaming.

The heat of the arc welder, the close confines of the workshop, and the sun through the open door had made the sweat roll off her body. She didn't mind. It felt good to focus on the immediate task. She had to. Flying droplets of flux covered the electrodes as they met the cold metal, but they could fly off and burn terrible scars into her if she were not careful. With her protective helmet in place and her hands covered in gloves that extended to her elbows, Nicole ran a clean, dense bead along the fractured edge of the wagon's tongue.

She worked feverishly until late afternoon and managed to finish welding the broken tongue back onto the wagon. She sat back on her heels and raised the visor of the helmet to check her work. The coating was even and there was no overlap. Sweat streamed down from her hair and was touched by a tiny breeze through the doors. The draft caused the sweat to evaporate in cooling chills under her drenched shirt.

"I need a break," Nicole said, rising to her feet and stretching her weary back.

At the cottage Nicole showered under the steaming hot streams of water until she was sure the sweaty salt had been banished from every part of her body. She reached out and swiftly turned off the hot water. Suddenly, she was under the stimulatingly brisk spray of cold water. She turned and let it revive her skin, front and back, until her teeth threatened to chatter. She stepped out of the shower and rubbed herself briskly with a large Turkish towel until her skin was pink and felt fresh. In the bedroom she put on a pair of clean blue jeans, T-shirt, socks, and comfortable boots. She grabbed her bedroll and walked into the kitchen. A few moments later she strolled out of the cottage, through the pasture gate, and toward the pond Jake had pointed out to her weeks before. With the bedroll under her arm and a lunch sack in her other hand, Nicole marched to the place she intended to claim as her personal retreat.

In less than two minutes she vanished from the view of the farmstead but not before Sally observed her disappearing around the barn and reappearing briefly as she made her way across the fields.

Nicole's feet took her over fallow meadows, across low meandering hills, and back toward the quiet solitude of the pond. On the last rise of the land, she navigated around the tilled and planted fields by staying close to the windbreaks of Scotch pine, cottonwood, and Russian mulberry groves.

As she walked the softened path on natural leaf mulch, she heard rather than saw the busy consternation of small furred creatures remarking about her invasion into their territory. Some chattered in protest as others swiftly vanished in flashes of fur into the shadowed depths of the windbreak.

Meeting the rise of the abbreviated hill, she immediately began her descent toward the edge of the pond. Western meadowlarks, a mockingbird, and two red-tailed hawks watched her from their flight as she walked through the tall grasses surrounding the pond.

As she stood at the edge of the pond, the only sounds she could hear were the lilting of breezes in the leaves of the oak and the thundering of her heart. She closed her eyes and felt the sun warm her face, heard the near noiseless lapping of the pond, and breathed in the rich sweet smell of the earth. She inhaled deeply and let the seclusion and silence of nature's liturgy fill her with pleasure.

She untied the bedroll and spread it out on the ground, dropping her lunch sack next to it. As she lay down on the spread she could hear the combination of brittle, winter-dried grasses and new sprouts crinkle under her weight. She lay there and let the heat and light of the sun play through her closed eyelids with their bright white radiance.

She sat up and reached for her lunch sack. In it she had placed sandwiches, an apple, and cheese with every intention of eating them. She didn't pull any of them out. Instead, she grabbed the bottle of inexpensive Chianti and quickly opened it.

Nicole took a long slow drink. She liked the feel and glow of it as it spilled down her throat and into her stomach. She liked it so much, she decided to have several more. For dessert, she extracted a tiny black cigar from a pocket in the sack, rolled it between her fingers, and deliberated about it as an overindulgence. Indulgence won. She found a crumbled pack of matches and slowly, with firm attention, held the flame a bare fraction of an inch from the cut tip. She inhaled slowly, coughed on the unfamiliar flavor, and took a drink of wine to aid in the digestion of the sharp flavor swirling in her mouth.

Nicole stretched out again on the outspread bedroll, content with herself and her little corner of the world. A gentle current of spring air flowed across the new grass and tickled her skin. The late afternoon sun soothed her and quieted her heart. The compact fragrances of the pond, meadow, and timber permeated her senses and she closed her eyes, drifting near sleep.

Languidly, Nicole snuffed out the half-smoked cigar and rose slightly to unbutton her blouse. The sun had grown hot against the material of the shirt, and she wanted the full benefit of the heat. She unbuttoned her cuffs and shrugged off the shirt and T-shirt to bare herself to the rays of the sun. She found the wine bottle, pulled the cork from its mouth, and drank deeply. As the red liquid flowed down her throat she lay back, shutting her eyes to everything but the overwhelming affirmation of her seclusion.

* * * * *

As Sally neared the pond she caught a glimpse of movement from the corner of her eye. A flash of plaid material and glimmer of skin on the other side of a patch of budding shrubs momentarily surprised her. She slowed her pace and warily walked toward the bushes. Apprehensively, tentatively, Sally leaned over the bushes and spied Nicole in slumbering repose. The swell of Nicole's breasts, coupled with the long smooth tone of her body, transfixed Sally's gaze and rekindled long buried hunger. Pulling her courage around her, she stepped around the thin shrubbery and softly cleared her throat as she emerged on the other side.

Nicole jumped at the sound of the dainty cough and quickly reached for her discarded shirt. Her eyes stared in trepidation, then widened in surprise as she recognized her visitor. Her hand forgot its mission and faltered in its search for her shirt. Amazed and uncertain, she watched Sally move through the rich green shoots of grass. Her light cotton dress moved as it clung to Sally's gentle curves. Nicole was speechless.

"Fancy meeting you here," Sally said as she knelt on the bedroll next to Nicole.

"Where did you come from?" Nicole managed to force the question from her throat.

"Over the hill and through the woods. Same as you. Except this used to be my favorite secret place. How did you find out about it?" Sally asked as she tried and failed to keep eye contact with Nicole.

"Sorry," Nicole said as she remembered her nakedness and made a hasty, blushing grab for the discarded clothes. As she tried to cover herself and recover the shirt, her hand hit the wine bottle and tipped it over. Sally deftly rescued the spilling bottle and just as quickly stalled Nicole's hand in its flight.

"This is supposed to be my place," Sally said teasingly as she raised the bottle to her lips.

"Jake showed it to me some time back. First week I came to work," Nicole responded as her heart tried to escape from her mouth.

"Hm, this does taste good," Sally remarked as she offered the wine bottle to Nicole. "You don't have anything dangerous or contagious, do you?"

"I've been tested and found healthy through and through," Nicole said, feeling the need to take another sip from where the lips she hungered for lingered a moment before.

"Me, too," Sally offered. "Never hurts to ask, does it?"

"No," Nicole said, feeling lightheaded on more than the wine.

"Will you share the rest with me?" Sally asked in sweet suggestion.

"If you stay here one more moment, the only thing I can promise you is that I can't promise to be on my best behavior," Nicole warned.

"You'd be bad?"

"I'd be as good as I know how. I can promise that," Nicole said as she reached over and cupped Sally's face gently in her hand. "It's best not to tempt someone with a sweet tooth," she admonished.

"There's a difference between teasing and tempting. Do you know what that is, Sergeant Jeager?" Sally asked as she kissed Nicole on the cheek.

"At this moment? I haven't a clue."

"Well, teasing is torment but tempting, that's

different . . . because it has follow-through," Sally said as she kissed Nicole full on the lips and moaned in sweet surprise as she drank in the taste of the full trembling lips on her mouth.

Rising to her knees, Nicole tenderly clasped Sally's shoulders and drew her into her arms. Their bodies met, and fires of the flesh lit where they touched. Blazing want seared into intense necessity. Nicole's mouth found and explored the nape of Sally's neck, the tip of her chin, and the hollow of her throat. Sally rose slightly on her knees and offered the small perfect globes of her breasts and felt herself freed from her bonds as Nicole unbuttoned the cotton shirtdress.

A tiny rivulet of sweat raced down Sally's neck between her soft, rounded breasts and hurried toward her navel. Nicole saw it, tried to catch it, to taste it on its swift, slick course. At Sally's moaned pleading, Nicole pulled at the dress, lifted its hem, and pulled it up over Sally's body. Freed from their restraint and the constraints of clothes, Nicole and Sally clung to each other, letting the full potency of flesh meeting flesh wash over them.

The caress composed Sally's mind and it became a clear pool of receptivity. They let the moment carry them closer to each other and to desire as their mouths opened in consuming duet. Sally moved against Nicole, asking with her body when words failed her. Nicole obliged and penetrated past her teeth to the wet, hot tongue that summoned her with flickering suggestions.

Sally wrapped her arms around Nicole's shoulders as she pressed her hands against Nicole's firm-fleshed back in urgency. With insistent fingertips, she begged

Nicole to flow through the barrier of flesh, to get closer, to meet and complete as one. She clasped her arms around Nicole's neck, arched her body at the entreating explorations of Nicole's hands, and opened herself to the new touch of love.

Slowly, as if there were no time, no place, no other moment that would ever exist, Nicole and Sally raced to the center of their worlds. Flesh, hearts, and souls touched and flowed together, straining in surrender one to the other. Where need touched, desire kindled fulfillment. Balanced in the moment they slowly moved down into sweet surrender under the sky.

Sally lifted her voice as her back arched in spasmodic tides of liberation. Her face buried in Nicole's neck, her muffled calls gushed in the quick cadence of gasping shock waves. Like plunging over Niagara Falls and being mysteriously saved from fatal shores by the rebounding of rippling tributaries, Sally's consummation coursed through her body.

Nicole whispered soft, love-shaded words to her, rocked her softly in her arms, and held her. She was happy, hungry still, but satisfied with the radiance she'd spread through Sally and shared in her own flesh.

They stayed by the pond loving and being loved until the sunlight was traded for shadows and the time came for them to go back to the farmstead.

On the walk home they touched hands, spoke quietly, looked expectantly at each other, and talked hesitantly about what they were feeling. Everything had changed. There was no more room for independent assumptions about the world. There had been a binding, but neither could speak as to what that might mean. They had no words yet for knowing. They shared one thing, a promise of hope in the days to come.

At the door of Nicole's cabin, Sally braved a kiss before leaving. They believed they were alone. Their interest in each other concealed Doug Harkner's shadow as it crossed the distance between the greenhouse and toolshed when he hurried from the field.

Chapter 9
Pests & Predators

Organic gardening or farming requires a balance. In the best of all situations, the use of sprays, dusts, and traps is unnecessary when the host of beneficial predators and parasites reaches a population where they can keep the number of damaging pests at a low or tolerable level. The determinant word in organic gardening is *tolerable*. *Tolerable* denotes a state of peaceful life activity for the creatures and bugs on the farm and in the garden where they keep them- selves in check. The only price you have to pay is the occasional nibble taken from a few crops. Organic gardening and farming requires a tolerance for minor losses to keep a ready supply of beneficial insects on hand.

Chemicals are antagonistic to the creation and maintenance of the delicate balance of life in nature and the organic garden. Even nontoxic, homemade concoctions can upset the balance in the soil as their application may pave the way for pest infestation. If you are attempting to maintain the peace and organic health of soil and plants, do not interfere with the damage until it becomes intolerable.

Prevention is the surest way to avoid insect trouble. Healthy plants and healthy soil are more able to withstand insect harassment than are weak plants.

An essential way of ensuring healthy pest-resistant plants is to make sure they get a balance of nutrients through the soil. The careful use of natural fertilizers should be maintained throughout the growing season. Use too much or too little, and you will encourage the pests to attack the luscious plants.

A variety of control mechanisms is available for the intently organic gardener: frequent cultivation, sanitation, planting times of specific plants that thwart their predators, mulching, crop rotation, plowing under infested plants, and many more. Knowledge of your predators and available plant control techniques is the organic gardener's best guide. Taking advantage of the natural life cycle of the pests is another tried-and-true method of preventing bug problems. After a few seasons of experience, you will notice that the same insects appear year after year and the times when they occur. They will live their short little lives and disappear until the next year or until the second brood appears in the same season. Steal the time between insect appearances to plant and harvest your crops before the pests enter their hunger stage. In your garden records, note the kinds of pests that cause the most trouble to the most plants and the time of the year when the damage becomes intolerable. Last but not least, an important tactic for the prevention of pests and the protection of the garden is companion planting.

Companion planting protects plants with other plants. This method has a number of ways to accomplish the intended benefit. All farms and gardens are better and healthier if they are not forced to endure or survive in a monoculture. Growing row after row or field after field of a pest's favorite life-sustaining substance is asking for trouble. The chance for infestation and the necessity of resorting to chemicals to save a crop may be avoided if different plants are grown every two or three rows. Interplanting and varying field plantings will reduce the infestation. Pests can be further discouraged when you intermingle plants that pests can't stand or tolerate with plants that they do like. One plant can protect and help the other; this is the key to companion planting.

Groundwork
Nicole and Sally became as inseparable as their busy work schedules could provide. They met in the

late afternoons of the days the restaurant was not open, the late evenings, and the early mornings before the sun came up. Infatuation, desire, and discovery embraced them, and care and caution slipped from their grasp. Old habits of distance and formality evaporated as they bared their lives and their bodies to each other.

When Sally was not with her, Nicole found herself thinking about her, wondering about the emotions and desire coursing through her mind. If a stray thought did slip in, it was to worry about the possibility of transience in Sally's gratifying passions. Nicole worked as hard as ever, but the memories of touch and passion playing in her mind overshadowed every task and sent involuntary thrills through her limbs. Unacquainted with the possibility of permanence in a relationship, the joy of their moments together disquieted her mind. Nothing and no one had ever endured beyond an allotted tour of duty. In the Army, she'd had the patent excuse of reassignment; orders and mandates from command had spared her all but the briefest regrets. She had never had to worry about constancy, stability, or the misery of regret and departure. So the worries tormented her, and as if they knew she was vulnerable, found her as she luxuriated in her lover's arms and frustrated her joy.

She was not used to having nagging concerns about her future or wanting a future with anyone. She wanted a future now. Nicole was the sole agent of her destiny, responsible for where she went, what she needed to do, and where she needed to go. But as free as she was, the arms and desires of another held her. The change in her thinking startled her and made her anxious for what she had never known she wanted.

Sally's every sensation, buried desire, and filament of repressed longing found expression in Nicole's arms. She coaxed long-forgotten memories to the surface and discovered herself.

Sally's mind, body, and soul took wing without fear or favor from the world. She knew what she wanted and what she had. In silent promises to herself, she let her desires bare themselves in deeds and compliant whispered words to Nicole. Sally silently promised to share her life and all the time that the universe might grant them together. She promised, knowing that a hundred years would be too little. Work and the running of the farm took on new meaning. They became the means and not the end for creating a life with love. She believed nothing could or would ever restrain her again.

As the days and weeks passed, Nicole's quandary plagued her unquiet mind, and Sally could regard nothing but the face of love before her. Nicole did not know how to share her apprehensions and hid them as best she could from herself. She had to. The guileless rare and open love she had never known that she missed reached for her at every opportunity. Sally's unabashed, hungering touch made her humble in its power.

* * * * *

A bit after three thirty-five in the afternoon, Gwynn Marian bounced off the steps of the school bus as it came to its scheduled stop at the end of the long driveway leading toward home. Like a freed prisoner, she squinted at the high June sun as she waved good-bye to other tiny passengers still captive in the yellow container. But summer school and the advanced computer class would be ending soon and she'd be free again until fall.

Gwynn Marian ran up the driveway and only fleetingly noticed the cars sitting in the parking lot of her mother's café. She dashed toward her house, intent on changing her clothes before she walked to the café to see if her mother needed any help.

Inside the house she ran up the stairs, shedding her school clothes as she went. In consideration for her mother, Gwynn Marian remembered to pick up her discarded garments and put them in the clothes hamper before running back down the stairs in her blue jeans and brightly colored blouse. As she raced out the door and into the bright warm air again, she grabbed her favorite hat off a peg on the porch to cover her copper-colored hair and protect her fair skin from overexposure to the sun. She hurried across to the café, feverishly hoping that her mother did not need her help. She wanted to saddle her pony and ride like the wind until it was time for supper.

Inside the restaurant she scooted past the tables where two propane-truck drivers sat discussing the merits of their occupation. She glanced at the corner table and noticed that Doug Harkner was talking to the banker. She grimaced and hoped her mother hadn't agreed to start dating the banker again. She knew he'd been pestering her. He'd been stopping and trying to get her attention for weeks. Gwynn Marian didn't like him. The feeling had seemed to be mutual from the first time they'd met. He had all too often expressed his opinion that children were a necessary evil and best kept out of sight. She frowned in his direction, but his conversation with Doug so engaged him that he failed to notice her as she passed by the kitchen doorway. She felt relieved. She didn't want to talk to him, either.

She sprinted through the wooden swinging door and almost collided with Martha in her haste to find her mother.

"Careful, girl," Martha chided.

"Sorry, Mrs. Marmer. Have you seen my mom?" Gwynn Marian asked when she noticed Martha was the only occupant in the kitchen.

"Not for an hour or so. And if you find her, would you tell her Mr. Bradley is looking for her?" Martha asked as she pulled two fresh rhubarb pies from the oven.

"What's he want?" Gwynn Marian asked poutingly as she pulled a milk carton from the refrigerator and tried to sneak some cookies off a baking sheet.

"Just came to visit, I guess. Now don't go ruining your supper," Martha scolded.

"You got eyes in the back of your head like my mother," Gwynn Marian said, putting back all but the one she popped swiftly into her mouth.

"Comes with age and raising children, dear. You'll know what I mean when you have your own,"

Martha said, chuckling at the wide-eyed expression on Gwynn Marian's face.

"See you later, Mrs. Marmer," Gwynn said as she raced out the back door and down the steps to where her pony waited. As she neared the corral, Gwynn Marian called to her pony, and he whinnied his hello back to her. She quickly saddled the little bay, mounted him, and headed for the distant rise of hills.

Her hair bounced and flew in the wind as she raced the pony over the dusty dirt and across the tilled fields. The thrust of wind swelled as she urged her pony in merry abandon to the long grasses of summer. She let the pony have his head as she hurried to her secret place. She'd hidden two plastic-wrapped books in the hollow of a tree. Half a mile ahead, near the rough outcrop of sandstone under the sheltering stand of elm, she would graze her pony and read again the enticing stories of *The Martian Chronicles*.

Popping over a gentle slope near the old pond, she prepared to turn her pony westward. A sudden flash of white toward the east distracted her. She thought she saw someone walking near the far tree line heading back in the direction of the house. Pulling the pony sharply up from his dash, she brought him to a halt. She looked toward the woods, but the figure had vanished into the shadows. She stared perplexedly at the woods and wondered if she'd imagined the whole thing.

Gwynn Marian turned in her saddle and started to nudge her pony back toward her intended goal. A startled yelp leaped in her throat as she realized someone was standing on the path in front of her.

"Miss Windrow," Nicole said evenly.

"You scared me," Gwynn Marian choked.

"That was not my intention," Nicole replied. "Are you supposed to be out here by yourself?"

"Sure," Gwynn Marian asserted with every ounce of her small dignity. "What are you doing out here?"

"If you must know," Nicole said as she reached for the pony's bridle to stroke his nose, "when I get tired of working, I walk to the pond down here and take a break. It's my private place, and I like to be there without being disturbed. Is that all right with you?"

"Of course. I have a secret place, too," Gwynn Marian confided.

"Then you know how I feel about it," Nicole affirmed.

"Sure, I do," Gwynn Marian asserted, making a mental note not to go to the pond unless she knew Nicole was still working. "So, my mom says she really likes you. You seem all right. I think it's nice you are her friend," Gwynn Marian continued cheerfully.

"Your mom is a very nice lady. I'm sure she has lots of friends," Nicole replied as she rubbed the pony's pink nose.

"Sure she does. She has lots of lady friends. I think some of them just come by to steal her recipes, but don't tell her I said that. She'll get mad. She used to like Mr. Bradley from the bank, but I never did. He talks too loud, and he tried to boss me around. Mamma dated him for a while, but I'm glad she stopped. You know, he told me that if he were my father, he'd see to it I got sent to a girls' school down in the Ozarks," she babbled without taking a breath. "He called it a finishing school. Said that was what little tomboys needed. Something about getting finished up. Doesn't matter, though. She says you're her best friend now," Gwynn Marian chattered.

Nicole smiled at the effusive young girl and glanced in the direction Sally had taken back toward the house. They'd managed to steal an hour together, and in spite of Sally's best intentions she had obviously missed getting back to the café before Gwynn Marian got home.

"I'd have to agree with you about Mr. Bradley. The idea of sending you away from your mother simply because he doesn't understand tomboys seems like a lame idea," Nicole commented.

"No kidding! I think that's why Mom stopped seeing him. He was always trying to butt into our business. Like he owned us or something," Gwynn Marian maintained.

Nicole refrained from chuckling as a look of pure indignation swept across the child's fresh face. "So where are you headed?" Nicole asked gently.

"To my secret place," Gwynn Marian responded in quiet tones.

"I see. Well, I think it's a fine thing to have a secret place. Everyone should have one. Just be careful with the pony and yourself. It wouldn't do to have any harm come to you."

"I'm careful," Gwynn Marian protested.

"Careful? Like riding this pony as though he had wings?" Nicole asked gently as she let go of the pony's bridle and stepped aside.

"I'll be more careful," Gwynn Marian promised, and she turned the pony to leave.

"That's the way."

"Nicole," Gwynn Marian said, stopping the horse and looking back. "Do you like my mom?"

"Yes. Very much."

"Good, because she told me she wants you to stay here always. Even if, even if Bill Cornweir gets well." Gwynn Marian smiled at Nicole. "I told her you could stay in the spare room next to mine," Gwynn Marian finished as she whipped her pony into a gallop.

Nicole watched the forthright innocent gallop off across the field and felt breathless at the guileless assertions of trust.

Nicole went back to her workshop and fairly whistled through her labors until seven-thirty that evening. She was exhausted but happy as she walked toward the cabin. She wanted a long hot shower and knew that her strained muscles would appreciate her efforts if she could manage to get to the cottage door.

As she rounded the corner of the hay barn, she saw Jake headed in her direction. He waved at her and motioned for her to follow him. She caught up with him as he climbed into the passenger seat of the deuce-and-a-half.

"What are you up to?" she inquired.

"Come on. Get in this rig. I forgot to go to town this morning and get feed for the critters," he declared.

"It takes two of us?"

"Does now, Sergeant. 'Sides, don't you want a bit of free time in town? You haven't set foot off this place in weeks. Come on, let's go blow some of the stink off. Better hurry, too. That feed store's likely to close iffen we don't hurry," Jake urged.

"Fine, fine. Give me a second," Nicole responded

as she walked around to the driver's door of the big truck. Settling into the driver's seat, Nicole realized Jake was right. She hadn't been anywhere, gone anyplace, or seen anything other than her unabridged need to be with Sally. What Jake suggested was reasonable and might do her some good. His offer for a little friendly conversation and company combined with their need to get the chores done was as good an excuse as any to go to town again.

Nicole reached out and turned the ignition of the truck. It sparked and sputtered. She released the key, pumped the gas, and let out the choke on the old truck. She tried again, and the truck coughed, strained, and finally turned over and came to life. "Remind me to take a look at the ignition system when we get back," Nicole said, laughing at the worried look on Jake's face.

"You got it," Jake said as they rolled toward town.

Jake seemed to fidget in silence as they approached the city limits. Nicole had been watching him for some time. She had known the old man long enough to be able to tell that something was on his mind.

"Spit it out, Jake, before you choke on it," Nicole braved.

Jake glanced in surprise at Nicole's announcement and went back to staring uncomfortably out the window. He lit a cigarette, inhaled, and let the blue smoke fill the cab. He took off his hat, scratched his head, and wiped invisible dust from the brim. Nicole's concern for what he was holding back grew as the long seconds ticked away.

"All right," he said finally. "The feed store is a

ruse." He turned to face Nicole as she frowned in apprehension. "Oh, don't look like that, we do need the feed and all. It's just that . . . it's . . . well, I figured it was time you and I had another snort together. See, there's this bar right across from the feed store. Kinda a favorite place of mine. I'm buying the first two rounds," he announced gallantly.

"That's it? That's the mystery you're fretting?" Nicole asked, feeling relief wash over her. She'd been apprehensive that something, someone, somehow might ruin or disturb the love she'd been reveling in. Healthy paranoia. That's what she'd called it in the Army, and nothing other than Sally's devoted attention was different in her mind in the civilian world.

"Sergeant, if there was anything else that I had been thinking, if there was anything I disapproved of," Jake said, "I'd tell you for sure. As it is, I'm as happy as a pig in shit."

"Is that a good thing?"

"It's a right good thing. You can bet your bottom dollar on that. The girl tells me you're the best thing that's happened to the farm and to her in years." Jake grinned widely at Nicole. "I'd call that a very right good thing."

"Then maybe I'll buy that first round," Nicole said, wondering if he had any idea what he was talking about but not inclined to enlighten him more than he was.

"No way in hell," Jake protested. "I'd said I'd buy the first two, and so I will. And I'll wrestle you for it if I have to, Sergeant."

"No need to, Jake," Nicole said as they pulled in

front of the feed store. "I wouldn't want you to embarrass me in public."

"Never happen, Sergeant. You have my word on that," Jake said as he climbed out of the truck and began yelling his needs to one of the workers standing on the dock.

Two hours later Nicole carefully drove the loaded two-and-a-half-ton truck back into the hay barn. On mutual agreement, Nicole and Jake decided not to try to unload the truck until morning.

The fire in the café started sometime after midnight.

Chapter 10
Garden Chaos

Mark Twain is credited with having said that if one doesn't like the weather in the Midwest, just wait a few days and it will change. And it does, like clockwork. To people who merely pass through the central plains, it's a curiosity as to why the natives spend so much time talking about the weather. It's not because there's a lack of conversational creativity. The truth is simpler and more pervasive than that.

Natives spend much of their time talking about the weather because there is so much of it.

Natives of the middle kingdom are acutely aware that all things, like the weather, shift. And the best way to prepare for shifting weather or fortune is to anticipate that everything has its place on the cycle, circle, or season.

Gardeners, and all women ever born, know that little truth the best. They have seen it in their labors and have noticed it in their lives. There is very little an astute observer of life might guarantee with unwavering certainty, other than that things will change. Like it or not, the effect of the weather is a matter of perspective. Helpful rain on one field harms another. Definitions of good or bad are more matters of opinion than fact. Sometimes the turbulence of change provides an opportunity to consider or reconsider the intentions and schemes that habit has made one become attached to.

Groundwork

By the time the county's volunteer fire department arrived at Windrow Garden, they found every able-bodied farmhand struggling to contain the fire. They were spraying down the blaze with every accessible garden and well-house hose they could get their hands on. The engine company joined them and worked furiously. The café flared as flames engulfed it, and they were barely able to keep the café's propane tank from exploding from the heat.

Four hours later, strained and soot-smeared faces

could be seen reflected in the orange glow of sunrise. The propane tank and the charred, shell-like remains of the café stood in mute testament to the night's struggle. The paramedics who had followed the fire trucks to the scene treated the firefighters for minor burns and smoke inhalation. Near the edges of the smoldering ruins, small clusters of weary firefighters and farm residents stood in motionless dismay.

Nicole, with her arm around Sally as Gwynn Marian clung to her mother, watched as the firefighters knocked down the smoldering remains of the café's walls. There was nothing to say. The devastation of the fire defeated any thought before it could be uttered.

Sally turned and looked up into Nicole's set jaws. "I don't know what we are going to do."

"Something," Nicole said holding her closer. "Something," she hoped fervently.

The state fire marshal and several deputy sheriffs showed up two days later. They asked Sally for permission to rummage through the fire in an attempt to find reason and cause behind the disaster. Sally quickly agreed, knowing that the insurance company would insist on speedy conclusions in order for her to recover from the loss. At the end of the day, a stern-faced fire marshal told Sally that he was unable to immediately determine the origin but felt fairly confident that a leaky gas line had been ignited by a pilot light.

Over the next six days following the fire, Nicole spent most of her time loading debris onto a flatbed wagon and hauling the mess of kindled wood to a pit in a nearby field. Ruined stoves, furniture, and refrigerators were hauled away by a local salvage yard. By the end of the week, with Jake's inter-mittent help, she had managed to have the area cleared of all but the scorched remains of the basement.

Work on the farm proceeded as best it could under the cloud of forlorn melancholy that pervaded every act. Nicole spent her evenings talking with Sally and entertaining Gwynn Marian as Sally tried to get the farm accounts to balance toward some kind of hope. After Sally would go to bed, weary, worn, and hopeless, Nicole would sit staring at the accounts and see the stark realization that immediate recovery was slim. It was an unhappy time.

Sally's mother, Gwynn O'Conners, arrived at the farm early the following Saturday morning and hours before the greenhouse was scheduled to open. She had no intention of starting work that early, but she had every intention of confronting what she saw as a hindrance to her daughter's happiness. She pulled her car in front of the greenhouse and, after locking it, squared her shoulders and walked determinedly toward Nicole's cottage. She was going to put her foot down. Sally was her daughter and she was determined not to let her throw her only chance of happiness away.

As Gwynn passed the window next to the cottage door, she glanced in and saw Nicole moving about the interior. Gwynn took a deep breath and pounded on the door. As it opened, she looked critically at the tall, solidly-built woman who stood blinking at her in surprise.

"Mrs. O'Conners?" Nicole asked in wonder.

"I need to talk to you," Gwynn responded stiffly.

Nicole watched the older woman's face. The woman's stern countenance sent a stab of dread through her. "Would you like to come inside?" Nicole asked uncertainly.

"No, not really, but I suppose it can't be helped," Gwynn O'Conners said as she strode inside the cottage.

Nicole stood watching in puzzlement while Gwynn O'Conners's hard little shoes marched noisily over the wooden floor and carried her equally rigid body into the room.

"What can I do for you?" Nicole asked, shutting the door.

Gwynn O'Conners turned around, and her glaring, mottled face hardened in her resolve. "You can stop bothering my daughter and my granddaughter. I want you to go away from here and leave them alone. And I want you to do it yesterday. That's what you can do for me," she said, letting the words fall in a smothering avalanche on Nicole.

"I'm not sure I understand —" Nicole sputtered in astonishment.

"Oh, I think you understand exactly what I mean. I don't have any idea what people are like where you come from, and I don't care. This simply won't be allowed. No, you won't be allowed to continue to come in here and corrupt my family. I'll see to that," she said as she raised her voice to ever sharper levels of belligerence.

"Mrs. O'Conners," Nicole began as she tried to keep her emotions under control, "I've not corrupted anyone. And I certainly have not bothered your granddaughter."

"It's just a matter of time. You and your filthy habits, your filthy mind, and your disgusting ways. You're trying to ruin my daughter, if you haven't already."

"I've done nothing —" Nicole began.

"The hell you haven't. What decent man would have anything to do with her after you've touched her? My God, it's a miracle that Donald Bradley would even think of having her, knowing what you might have done!" Gwynn raged as she stood rigidly in the center of the room as though the air itself might contaminate her.

"Mrs. O'Conners," Nicole began again under the stinging onslaught, "I suggest you speak with your daughter. And regardless of what you might think, I am not a monster," Nicole fumed as she struggled to respond without letting herself walk over and slap the woman.

"The hell you aren't. Bradley's shared . . . told me . . . told me . . ." the woman choked into silence.

"What could he say? What could he ever fathom to say to you? And why would he want to make you so obviously disturbed and angry?"

"To save my daughter!" Gwynn retorted. "He knows what he's talking about, all right. He's not a stupid man. He obviously has his ways of finding things out. But it really doesn't matter. It's nothing more than I suspected about you. He simply confirmed what I already feared to be the worst."

"I —" Nicole began.

"Don't you, don't you dare say a thing," Gwynn

said, cutting Nicole off. "I want my daughter to be happy again. I want her free from this ugly taint, and I want you out of here. Bradley doesn't hold it against her. He knows she's been lost and lonely. Easy pickings for some predatory creature like you. You took advantage of her, but you're not going to have your way one more second, if I have anything to say about it!"

Nicole's head swam under the vicious attack and vile accusations directed at her by the delicate looking woman. She slowly raised her hand to stop the abuse. "Your daughter's happiness, whatever you think that might mean, is her business, Mrs. O'Conners. Not your business and not Bradley's. She's an adult. Don't you think she knows her own mind?"

"I do not. Because you've twisted and confused her. You're the one to blame here. Not my daughter. I bet you started laying your nasty little trap for her the minute you arrived here. I've heard all about your kind before. You prey on weakness, susceptibility, and vulnerability. You're a scavenger, Miss Jeager. A hideous, contemptible scavenger."

"I'm going to ask you to leave," Nicole said as she deliberately turned her back on the woman and opened the cottage door. She had to get the woman out of her house. If she didn't get her out quickly, Nicole knew she would say things to Sally's mother that she might regret later, and things that could harm Sally's relationship with her mother.

"Oh I'll leave, but not before you know how precious little time you have left here. You're going. Mark my words. Bradley has been doing some checking. He has a friend at Fort Leonard Wood. It seems that you left the Army with a bad taste in its mouth," Gwynn said smugly.

"If you do that, if you have him come after me, you'll end up hurting your daughter. Think how your actions would affect her and Gwynn Marian. Why would you do that if you love her as much as you say?" Nicole ventured in shock.

"To save her. To save her from you. To make sure that she gets a real man, a good man to love and marry, to do things for her that you'd obviously never understand," Gwynn spewed.

"I'm not a man. I am a woman, and I don't want damage to come to your daughter, regardless of what you might think. And take *this* warning back to your banker friend: He can come after me all he wants, but if he dares to hurt either Sally or her daughter, I'll make him wish he'd never been born."

"Good. He loves a challenge, but then I don't think you can trouble a real man like that. We're in agreement, then?"

"Hardly," Nicole swore.

"But I th-thought —" Gwynn O'Conners stuttered.

"You've been doing far too much thinking by what I can see," Nicole warned. "Thing is, you haven't had the decency to hear your daughter out on this matter. As I said, she's a grown woman, and she knows her own mind. I'm not sure she would appreciate your trying to run her life at this late date."

"You're right. But if you step aside, and let love, not your unnatural lust, have an opportunity, I think you'll see that Sally doesn't need you or want anything to do with your kind."

"You think so?" Nicole retorted as sensations of uncertainty raised their nauseating little heads in her psyche.

"I'd be willing to put money on it. Or would you like some money now to encourage you with your packing?"

"No, I would not. Not now or ever," Nicole responded as vague fears crept through her shoulders. What she was suggesting was probable. Sally had been basking in the glow of love and lovemaking. It was a far cry from the hateful, disparaging treatment she might receive at the hands of a community turned against her. The fear of losing her business, customers, and the farm, Nicole reasoned, might be enough to scare Sally back into the deepest closet imaginable. Nicole knew from Sally how she had hidden her yearnings away before. She knew how she'd locked them away to embrace the safety and security of convention. The threat of certain reprisal, Nicole worried, could be the trigger that would send her into hiding again.

Nicole swallowed hard and let her anger seep into her voice. "You have a hard, mean-spirited little heart, Mrs. O'Conners."

"I'm a mother, Miss Jeager. All mothers have sharp teeth. Although I'm sure it's not something someone like you would know."

"You don't know me," Nicole responded.

"Maybe not, but I certainly know all I care to. I think you're a coward and you're afraid my daughter will come to her senses."

"Mrs. O'Conners, I'm not afraid of any decision your daughter makes."

"Then back off. Give my daughter breathing

space, time to think, and time to come to her senses. This isn't the first time she's flirted with someone like you. That was a mistake. This, this is a phase, and nothing more in a lonely woman's life. And if you're not the coward you say, you'll give her the freedom to choose. I think you'll be amazed how quickly and ravenously she'll reach out for the chance at a normal happy life. You're no comparison to what Bradley would give her."

"That would be a fair statement," Nicole conceded as she bit her tongue to keep the words of love she felt for Sally from passing her lips.

"Now," Gwynn O'Conners announced as she walked to where Nicole was holding the door open, "if you'll get out of my way, I've got work to do. I just pray that you can find it in your heart to do what you know is right."

As Gwynn O'Conners walked through the door, Nicole called after her. "What if she chooses to be with me?"

Laughing, Gwynn O'Conners called back to Nicole over her shoulder, "Why, I'd have to learn to live with it, wouldn't I? But I know my daughter, and you would stand a better chance of getting ice water in hell than for that to happen."

As a growing sense of disquiet began to plague her mind, Nicole watched Mrs. O'Conners stalk to the greenhouse.

Chapter 11
Taste & Temperament

Herbs — the whole plant or, in many instances, parts of the plant (stem, leaves, roots, berries) — provide the pleasure of fragrance and other comforts for the body and the psyche. The broader definition of *herb* includes trees, shrubs, and herbage. The naive gardener is cautioned. Although many books on the market attest to the ingestible benefits of herbs, no herb raised in your own garden should be used without a thorough knowledge of its effects and dosage.

Some of the easiest to grow and the most practical herbs offer both pleasure and medicinal benefit: comfrey, coltsfoot, peppermint, garlic, rosemary, catnip, chamomile, sage, horseradish, shallot, parsley, fennel, dill, chive, and cayenne.

You do not have to feel poorly to use herbs. Herbs provide interesting additions to culinary efforts. Experimentation with sprinkling, rubbing, or simply adding fresh or dried herbs to traditional entrées, soups, and breads may provide an extraordinary revival of pleasure and interest in an otherwise simple meal. Experiment with care. Only add a little at a time so as not to alarm diners or overreach preferences of taste. Too much too soon might make future guests less eager to return to your table.

There are a multitude of reasons to add herbs to your garden. It's not simply a matter of providing delectable differences at mealtime. Herbs, because of their variety, also add colorful tones and fragrances to the space you've devoted to your gardening labors.

Herbs are often used as companion plants to assist in the protection of nearby crops. You will want to do research to discover which herbs provide the best companionship with what varieties of fruits and vegetables.

For starters, it is best to grow herbs organically, on a small scale, and develop one's habits of harvest and drying before attempting quantity production. Herbs will thrive in soil that would normally be considered too harsh for typical fruits and vegetables. They can thrive on the smallest amount of nutrients but also appreciate well-drained and enriched soil. Naturally resistant to insects, hardy herbs can be expected with the tiniest bit of tender loving care.

Herbs can be yearlong companions when you know them, grow them, use them, and preserve them. They will add much to the garden and home. You will come to appreciate them for their blushing and vivid colors, their savory ambience, and their evocative fragrances.

Groundwork

Mrs. O'Conners managed to divert Sally's attention from Nicole, and Sally became remote to everyone and everything. Her conversations with Nicole were infrequent and dealt with her worries over the future of the farm. She evaded Nicole's hints and suggestions that they go somewhere and talk, insisting that she was too busy to be diverted from her tasks. Nicole's mood grew grim the first evening she noticed Bradley's car parked in front of Sally's house.

Nicole absented herself from the farm for several days the following week. She would leave early in the morning and not return until late in the afternoon. She would go to the machinery sheds and work until late in the evening. She kept up the feverish pace and absented herself from mealtimes.

There were plans afoot. Ideas she had been generating and investigating were coming together. All she needed and wanted was an opportunity to tell Sally the things she'd found out, the things she could arrange for, and to help make the farm whole again.

She was willing to invest time, money, sweat, and tears to stay with Sally and be part of her life. If that was what Sally wanted. But first she needed the opportunity to talk with Sally, and that possibility seemed more remote than ever.

Her heart was like a weight in her chest whenever she had reason to go to the greenhouse. Replacing several yards of corroded copper pipelines along the baseboards took several days worth of effort. Mrs. O'Conners never spoke to her; she insisted on ignoring her. The smirk on the old woman's face seemed to say everything Nicole could not bear to hear aloud. Swayed, chastised, or coerced by her mother, Sally seemed to have receded into a frosty indifference.

Two weeks later, on a Wednesday evening, when Nicole pulled into the driveway of the farm, she saw a black Le Sabre sitting in front of Sally's house again. Her heart dropped as anger provoked her. She dropped the truck in gear and roared up the drive before coming to a skidding halt next to the vehicle.

With her pulse racing and temples pounding, she managed with every ounce of her self-control not to rush into Sally's house and confront Sally with her banker. In a moment's worth of reflection, she realized she did not know what she would say to him or Sally without being reduced to tears.

Anger overwhelmed her and was immediately replaced by a sense of loss deeper than she ever knew she could feel. What could she say to Sally? What difference would it make? Her shattering heart told her that Mrs. O'Conners had been right. She was nothing more than an interloper into Sally's otherwise secure life. She saw herself as an anomaly in the acceptable society in which Sally lived. And then she understood how the fire drove Sally back to her old securities.

Frustration coursed through her body. She gripped the steering wheel until her knuckles felt as though they would crack under the pressure. She trounced on the gas and gunned the engine.

Nicole stormed into her cottage and headed for the kitchen. She pulled a bottle of bourbon from under the counter and poured herself a tall drink. The first taste shocked her throat, making her choke as angry tears sprang to her eyes.

Her immediate inclination was to pack her bags, load her tools, and leave the farm before sunset. But she knew it was her outrage seeking release, and she knew she wouldn't do it. She'd never walked away from a fight in her life. And win or lose, she wasn't going to start now. The second swallow of bourbon eased her pounding head as she reminded herself that leaving would only further complicate Sally's life. Bill Cornweir would not be able to return to work for several more months. If she left, she might destroy Sally's opportunity to keep the farm operational. Leaving would be an act of betrayal. It would violate her lifelong code of ethics.

Nicole walked over to the sink and poured the remaining glass of bourbon down the drain. She didn't want any more. She knew what she needed to do. It didn't matter to her that her hopes and dreams might never come about. What did matter, she realized, was that she do what she had promised Sally in the first instance. She would manage the equipment and do what needed to be done until Bill Cornweir returned. She bit back the tears as she headed out the door to the solitary comforts of the lonesome pond.

Later that evening, as Nicole worked under the glare of a bare bulb in the machine shed trying to tighten the tension of a mower's idler pulley, she heard movement behind her. She turned around to see Sally walking toward her with a pot of coffee and a plate of sandwiches. As she laid down her wrench, Nicole tried to keep her heart from racing and her hands from trembling.

"You didn't come to supper, so I thought I'd bring supper to you," Sally said nonchalantly as she motioned to Nicole.

"I'm not very hungry," Nicole said. She started to turn back to her work.

"I know what you mean. I've had a little difficulty trying to find the energy or desire to eat lately myself," Sally said, placing the plate of sandwiches on a workbench.

"Your banker friend not much company?" Nicole asked and immediately regretted it. She didn't want to fight with Sally, and a war of words would be too easy to sink into. "Sorry."

"Oh, that's fine. I didn't realize you'd come back before he left," Sally said innocently. "But now that you ask, he had a very good reason for leaving early. I kicked him out."

"How so?" Nicole puzzled aloud, feeling a twinge of hope surface.

Sally poured coffee into the two mugs she'd brought and handed one to Nicole. "You know," Sally began, "sometimes that man makes me so mad I could spit. The bastard stopped by, bringing what he called good news and bad news."

"What's the bad news?" Nicole asked hesitantly. The last thing Sally needed was more bad news. She figured she knew the good news for Sally but couldn't bring herself to ask.

"The bad news is that he'd been talking to Bill Cornweir. Seems as though Bill and his girlfriend Sheila Ray intend to get married."

"That doesn't sound bad, leastways for them," Nicole offered.

"It does when you consider the fact that my friendly banker has helped him find a new job," Sally said as her lips trembled.

"He found him a job?"

"Sure as hell did," Sally bristled. "Behind my back, knowing that I'd expected him to come back to work. Said he'd been working on it with Bill for a month or more. Then he said it was in my best interests and that it gave us an opportunity to make new plans."

"How . . . how did he figure that?" Nicole asked as she readied her heart to hear what she'd been fearing for weeks.

"He proposed. Said we'd make a great team and that he'd see to it that I'd never have to work again," Sally said as she struggled to look Nicole in the face.

"I see," Nicole responded, swallowing hard.

"No, you don't, not yet," Sally asserted. "That lousy little son of a bitch told me he had plans for the farm. Plans that would make us rich. Things like selling the farm, running a highway through here, and cutting the rest of it up into little pieces for tract housing!" Sally exclaimed, quivering with anger.

"My farm! Our farm! The son of a bitch wants to destroy our farm!"

Our farm? Nicole wondered. "And, you don't want to?"

"My God, no! I've never wanted that, and I sure as hell don't want to marry him! It never crossed my mind."

"You didn't . . . I mean you don't?"

"No, not either one," Sally announced, looking up into Nicole's eyes. "I never wanted that. He was a friend. That was all. Oh, and a banker, that's why I've been talking to him. I was concerned about the mortgage I'd taken out. It paid for the café, but we know what happened to it. Anyway, I needed some time to think and find out if we were going to be in any serious trouble with the place. I haven't been able to eat, sleep, or drink without it preying on my every waking moment. Of course, now I find out just how much of a friend he was. We used to go to dinner . . . I suppose he always had an idea for more in the back of his head," Sally said and then frowned. "No, I take that back. I can see now what kind of an idea he had in the back of his head. And it pisses me off. I kicked him off the property."

"How did he take that?"

"Let's just say he wasn't too happy. We got into a bit of a shouting match. The warty little weasel tried to intimidate me. Imagine! He said I'd be sorry. I can't imagine being any sorrier than if I had ever remotely considered life with him. That is not what I want."

"What do you want?" Nicole dared.

Sally put down her coffee cup and walked around

159

the workbench to where Nicole stood gripping her cup as though it might fly.

"You," Sally said softly. "I want you, and I want us to make this farm work. I want you by my side. I want you in my life, and I don't ever want to hear about you wanting anyone other than me," she cooed as she took the cup from Nicole's hands.

"One thing for sure. You're going to have to get better about talking to me when things bother you," Nicole cautioned.

"I know . . . I promise. This is the last time I let my fears and confusion keep us apart," Sally said as she held out her arms.

Nicole opened her arms and wrapped them tightly around her as Sally glided into them. "You sure you aren't just looking to keep the only mechanic you have?" Nicole bantered lightly against the release of her fear. She kissed Sally's cheek.

"I can find a mechanic anywhere. What I couldn't find, didn't know I needed to find, was you and what I've been wanting all of my life. Can you handle that?"

"Then we really have things to talk about," Nicole said as she bent her head down to kiss Sally's expectant mouth.

"We certainly do," Sally responded. She returned the fevered pitch of the kiss Nicole tendered.

"Careful," Nicole said, coming up for air. "If you keep that up, I won't be held responsible for what happens next."

"It is late," Sally commented with a smile. "I suppose Gwynn Marian can spend the night by herself in the house. She's a big girl. What say you and I spend a little quiet time alone."

"As you wish," Nicole said.

"It's been too long. We have a lot to talk about."

"Talking would be one thing. I have some things and plans of my own that I'd like to share with you."

"Is that what you call it?" Sally replied, laughing as Nicole hugged her with all of her might.

"Good as any. I cleaned my cottage today. Would you care to inspect the premises?"

"Well," Sally said, looping her arm through Nicole's, "it's either there or here, and I've been missing you so . . . here looks pretty good, too."

"No, really. I've been working on some things and didn't want to tell you until I had everything worked out. There may be a way for you to continue doing some of the things you did best at the restaurant but without having to work fifteen and twenty hours a day to get it done. I mean, if you want to. And you don't have to wait for the insurance money to do it," Nicole said as she escorted Sally to the cabin.

"I don't understand," Sally confessed.

"I'll explain. It could be a wild and harebrained idea, but I wanted an opportunity to see what you think about it. It is your farm, so it is really your decision."

"This doesn't have anything to do with selling all or part of the farm does it?" Sally asked tentatively.

"Not a bit, but it would make us partners in more ways than one," Nicole cautiously approached the proposal.

"Then I'd love to hear it," Sally said. "But could we wait until I get you in bed?"

"Absolutely," Nicole said, smiling fiercely.

At two o'clock the next morning, Nicole gently slid out of bed as she tried not to disturb Sally's slumber. Something had disturbed her sleep. She lay still, listening and watching. Nothing but the sound of a light wind whistling through the trees came to her ears. Restlessly, she turned to Sally and, seeing her face in the moonlight, whispered her devotion.

The first moment of wakefulness sent her mind racing with the ideas and hopes she and Sally had shared earlier. After making love and making love again, Nicole had told Sally about her ideas. She told her about the savings she'd acquired, the discussions with a Realtor about a small house that needed to be moved from its current location, and the costs of setting it up on the basement of the burned-out restaurant. She told Sally about spending her days down in Kansas City, Missouri, with store owners, restaurateurs, and health-food consortia. Nicole explained how the ideas could fit together in a way that could get the farm back on its feet and satisfy her love of cooking.

Sally had been very receptive to the ideas that Nicole had shared with her. She liked the idea of creating an organic bakery, leasing a building space at the River Market, and combining her love for cooking with creations from the farm for people and businesses in Kansas City. They both knew it was a long shot, that it would take hard work and dedication; but they felt the risks were worth it and there was nothing to lose if they stood together.

Before she'd fallen asleep, Sally was planning the types of cheesecakes she'd bake along with the pesto she'd create to sell with the produce and bottled herb oils and vinegars for the shop. She'd talked about buying a new computer, going online to offer baskets of fresh, seasonal organic delights to the customers she could develop and the contacts Nicole had made at the River Market. This would provide an opportunity to stay in business and reduce the overall hours Sally spent working.

The ideas leaped and swirled in Nicole's mind again. In resignation, Nicole knew that sleep was not going to be immediately possible and quietly crept out of bed.

She grabbed a T-shirt, wriggled into it, and headed for the kitchen. Her step was light as she skipped across the floor. Thoughts of work and the plans they spoke of were quickly replaced by the sweet memories of the other gifts Sally had bestowed on her that evening. She was almost tempted to return to the bedroom and see if she could lovingly coax Sally awake.

Nicole reached into a drawer and pulled out a small black cigar. Her mind and heart were racing with the possibilities of life with Sally and the opportunities that faced them. She sneaked back into the bedroom and quietly grabbed her blue jeans and returned to the living room to put them on. She could not quiet her mind, and she worried that the smell of the tiny cigar might wake Sally. She walked outside to have her indulgence in the dark.

Nicole stepped into the shadows and looked up into the sky at the full bright moon. Her heart swelled anew for the luck and love she felt. The warm summer air drifted past her and wafted the smoke from her cigar across the compound.

As Nicole stood under the broad shadow of the elm tree, she heard the soft, hurried sounds of footsteps near Sally's house. She peered into the darkness and wondered if one of the animals had broken out of its pen. Then she saw a thin, hunched form emerge from the shadows by the house and move cautiously into the full light of the moon. It was no farm animal. At first she thought it was Jake, that his age-induced intermittent sleep habits had made him as restless as she was this night. She almost called out but was immediately thankful when the words stuck in her throat.

The figure hurried past the orchard and headed in the direction of the machine shop with agility and speed that Jake did not possess. A siren of panic shot through her. Everything about the furtive movements told her that whoever it was, the person meant no good. Nicole quickly snuffed out her cigar on the bark of the tree and ran barefoot across the yard toward the hurrying shadow before her.

Years of military training fresh in her body and mind came on full alert as she crouched in the shadows, listened, and then ran to the corner of the shed. She squinted her eyes to try to pierce into the darkness through the window. A soft thud from the interior made her pull her head away from the glass. The sound told her all she needed to know. Someone, someone who shouldn't be there, was inside. She crept around to the west end of the long shed and worked her way toward the opening in the double doors. Her palms itched for want of a weapon, and she searched the ground near the doors for something to use.

Suddenly, the sound of hurrying footsteps rattled in the shed. Whoever was inside was coming back toward the doors. He stopped just inside the darkened opening. Nicole froze into position as the man waited and searched the farmstead for movement.

As Nicole listened to his attempts to calm his struggled breathing, she realized that apprehension had clouded his perceptions. Her crouching form in the long shadow of the shed rendered her invisible even though she could almost have touched him if she'd raised her arm.

He emerged slowly. First his head and neck, then his shoulders, until he finally stepped into the night. He stopped and waited again before making his next move.

It was all the time Nicole needed. She shifted in her crouch, used her hands for balance, and lashed out with her feet. Her jackknifed legs coiled for the jolting strike.

At the sound of her movement, the man turned his head in her direction, but it was too late. Nicole's leg muscles snapped in their powerful springing motion. Her feet landed with a hard, crunching impact into the man's hip.

"Unnghh!" exclaimed the injured man as he was tossed into the air. The trajectory of the blow sent him crashing down onto the gravel driveway.

Nicole bounded to her feet and fell on the man in fury. She pummeled him until his struggling subsided. She stopped her pounding, and at that moment he made a grab for her. Quickly and smoothly, she snatched his left arm and twisted it violently up behind his shoulder blade. He screamed and pleaded for her to stop.

"Please, oh God, stop!" he cried.

"Doug?!" Nicole asked in surprise when she recognized the man's voice. "What the hell are you doing out here?" she asked as her head turned to look back into the interior of the shed.

"Christ, lady, don't . . . you're breaking my arm."

"And it'll stay broke," Nicole warned as she seized him by the scruff of his shirt and hauled him up to his feet. She twisted his wrist and kept the pressure on the arm in a sharp, upward hold. She had no intention of letting him wriggle out of her grasp. The hold would also keep him from contemplating any stupid moves on his part.

"Now," she said as she shoved him back toward the cottage. "What the hell are you doing sneaking around this place?"

"He put me up to it . . ." Doug Harkner sputtered as Nicole marched him toward the cottage.

"Who? What are you talking about?" Nicole asked as the first whiff of smoke reached her nose. "What the —?" Nicole began as her head snapped towards Sally's house. A wave of thick, flickering orange and blue flame shot up the side of the wall. "You son of

166

a bitch!" Nicole yelled as she shoved Doug's face into the side of the cottage door.

Doug collapsed into a heap as Nicole flung him through the open door. She raced inside the cottage to the kitchen while yelling at Sally to wake up. When she couldn't lay her hands immediately on what she wanted in the kitchen drawers, she ran to her reading lamp in the living room. Nicole ripped the cord from the wall and tore it from the base of the lamp in desperation. She called to Sally again, fear and alarm strengthening her voice. Quickly returning to Doug's unconscious heap, she tied him securely and dragged his body over to her parked truck.

Sally came stumbling out of the cottage door as Nicole finished lashing the remaining portion of the cord high and tight to the truck's bumper.

"What the hell's going on?" Sally demanded sleepily.

"Call nine-one-one. Your house is on fire," Nicole snapped.

"Oh my God," Sally wailed. "Gwynn Marian!"

"I'll get her. Call for help," Nicole said as she bounded across the yard. "Hurry!"

Nicole raced toward the house, heedless of the large sharp stones of the driveway. She opened the front door of the house and almost collided with Gwynn Marian coming out.

Nicole grabbed her and hugged her fiercely. "Are you OK?"

"I was, but I think you cracked a rib. What's all the yelling about?"

"The house is burning, at the back. Go to your

Mom. She's at the cottage. Quickly! She needs you," Nicole commanded. She ran toward the side of the house where she'd seen the flames. As she rounded the corner, she tripped over an idle cold frame and fell. Her arms jerked out in front of her to protect her. As she landed, she heard and felt a wrenching in her right arm and snap in her wrist.

Nicole sat up, clutching her injured arm and shutting her stinging eyes against the pain. In the distance she could hear Sally raising the alarm, screaming for Carl, Martha, and Jake to wake up. The sense of urgency made Nicole rise to her knees and try to stand. She looked at the cold frame that had sabotaged her and saw in the glow of the flames the well pipe stand that Sally used to water the seedlings.

She lunged toward it. With her good left arm, Nicole twisted the faucet handle open to full force. She looked around for the hose end. It sputtered and sprayed to life under her feet, and she grabbed at the nozzle and aimed it toward the spreading fire. The two-inch hose jerked and bucked in her grasp as she struggled to subdue the fire.

The strain caused sharp barbs of pain to spike viciously into her wrist and jolt her wounded shoulder. She gritted her teeth and hung on. As the flames began to drown under the onslaught of the stream of water, Nicole sank to her knees. Suddenly, Sally and Carl Marmer were at her side.

"Gwynn Marian?" Nicole asked as Carl took the hose from her grasp.

"Jake's got her. She's safe now," Sally said as she wrapped her arms around Nicole.

"Ahhggh," Nicole cried out as Sally grasped her

injured shoulder. "I've done something to my arm," she complained.

"What?"

"A combination of good intentions and clumsy feet, I think," Nicole said, wincing.

"We'll get it looked at. It's all right. Everything is going to be all right now. We're safe," Sally said as sirens cut through the night.

Chapter 12
Home & Hearth

An arbor is more than a laced wooden support for grapes or other vine plants. With a little creativity, conscious design, and effort, an arbor can support whatever vine shade you wish to grow and provide a secluded place of privacy. To catch privacy and the cooling breezes of summer, place the open ends so that they offer a natural flow of the predisposed winds. However, if you would enjoy something more elaborate, U, T, or C shapes are also popular.

As in all things related to the garden, the development of a comfortable shaded arbor is a matter of patience and effort; a minimum of two years will be required to ensure a leafy haven. Arbors are relatively easy to construct but should consist of sturdy, well-sunk posts topped with wooden lattice-work. Make sure to build the arbor wide enough to allow passage and/or lounging on those hot summer afternoons and nights. You should build the arbor a minimum of eight feet wide and seven feet high. The length of the arbor would be a matter of taste and space available.

An arbor can provide a wonderful withdrawal to bright foliage and fresh berries. A sweet retreat, it makes a pleasurable and well-earned reward for your labors.

Groundwork

On Monday of the following week, as Sheriff Cook pulled his car into the long driveway of Windrow Garden, he could see the bright yellow cab of the Bashor City Lumber Company backed up to the west side of Sally Windrow's house. He smiled to himself at the endurance and fortitude of the people he was pleased to serve. He had good news for the residents of the tiny hilltop community, and he'd made sure that he was the one to deliver it.

Alighting from his patrol car, Sheriff Cook walked around to the side of the house and spotted Sally talking to the woman he'd been introduced to the night of the fire as Nicole Jeager. He watched as they stood close together, discussing the invoice of materials the wranglers were off-loading from the lumber truck, and he recalled the rumor that had filtered through town. He shook his head, reminding himself that some things were not his concern, and hailed the two women.

"Sheriff Cook?" Sally said, turning toward the direction of a voice calling her name. She smiled quizzically at him as he approached. "What are you doing out here? You know I don't have any bakery goods for you anymore," she chided.

"Well now, that's a real shame, but it never hurts to check on these things. Good morning to you, Ms. Jeager," he said to the woman standing next to Sally as he nodded his hat.

"Sheriff," Nicole acknowledged. "Is everything all right? Or is this a social call?"

"More than right. I've got some very good and interesting news for you," he said as he pulled a small notebook from his breast pocket.

"Would you like to speak to Sally, alone?" Nicole offered.

"No, you can be here, too. I mean if it hadn't been for your tackling that ol' boy last week and trussing him up for us, the whole scheme might never have unraveled. So this involves you," he affirmed.

"Involves her how, Sheriff?" Sally asked.

"Just this. Seems as though that hired hand Ms. Jeager trounced so soundly was pretty anxious not to take the fall for everything by himself. You remember, he told Ms. Jeager here that someone had put him up to it?"

"Nicole, Sheriff. Yes, I mentioned it to one of your deputies the night of the fire," Nicole responded.

172

"Nicole then, ma'am. Well, when he found out that he was about to be charged with two counts of felony arson — aggravated assault on your child, Ms. Windrow, because she was in the house when he torched it, and assault and battery on you, Nicole — he decided he wanted to share a lot of information," Sheriff Cook said as he flipped through the notebook.

"Who was he working for?" Sally asked.

"You won't believe it in a hundred years. I know I didn't, not at first, but when we brought him in, he just broke down like a cheap shotgun," Sheriff Cook said, grinning widely at them.

"Who, Sheriff?" Nicole insisted.

"Donald Bradley from the bank. I understand he was your gentleman friend, Sally?"

"Not exactly. We kept company sometimes. And if what you say is true, he's certainly no friend of mine," Sally fumed. "Why in the world would he do something like that?"

"I thought that's what you'd say. About him not being your friend and all. Seems he's pretty much of the same idea. As to why he did it, why he encouraged you to hire Doug and put a snake in your garden, well, that's a little complicated," Sheriff Cook said, raising an eyebrow.

"Complicated, how?" Nicole encouraged.

"It seems as though he had a couple of motives for wanting to hurt you and ruin your farm, Sally. At the moment, he's madder than hell. Way he tells it, he's a jilted lover. Seems as though he's under the impression someone was beating his time," Sheriff Cook said as he glanced from Sally to Nicole.

Nicole cleared her throat and gazed steadily back at the Sheriff. "You mean to say that he had Sally's restaurant burned, set fire to her house, and threatened her child's life because he was jealous? That's crazy."

"It sure is crazy sounding, but I figure he's sane enough to stand trial. Of course, his jealousy doesn't cover everything. Seems the whole idea of getting Sally here in a weak and compromised position with the farm had been on his mind for a long time. And we arrested a third fellow yesterday who we believe to be a part of what's turning out to be a major conspiracy against Windrow Garden and quite a few others around here. He's been a very busy boy."

"Sheriff, I think I'd like to have some coffee and sit down while I hear the rest of this," Sally said, her mind a whirl of confusion and wonder. "Let's go into the house, shall we?"

"Be my pleasure, ma'am. You wouldn't happen to have any of those delights you used to bake in there, would you?" he asked, grinning shyly.

"I think I might be able to find something," Sally said as she and Nicole escorted the sheriff inside.

An hour later, Sheriff Cook waved good-bye to Sally and Nicole as he patted a bag of six slices of perfect cheesecake on the car seat next to him. He'd promised her he would share the toffee cream delights with the rest of his staff. It had been a white lie he knew he could afford. He pulled out of the drive and back on to the highway, musing about the detailed paperwork on the case he hoped his detectives were seeing to completion.

Nicole, Sally, and Gwynn Marian stood together watching the sheriff's car roll down the hill. Their surprise, wonder, and astonishment at what the sheriff had revealed of the plot against Windrow Garden was still etched across their faces.

Nicole shook her head as she turned to Sally. "I think that's one of the most deceitful and greedily malicious things I've ever heard of anyone doing. I mean, I knew I didn't like Bradley, but I had no idea I had a real good reason to hate the man."

"You?" Sally chuckled ruefully at the thought of Donald Bradley trying to wine, dine, and bed her to steal her farm from her. "He was loathsome, and he almost got away with it. Him and that highway guy, whatever his name is. I hope they rot," Sally fumed.

"Can the state still build the highway, Mom?" Gwynn Marian asked worriedly as fearful concern traced across her fresh youthful brow.

Sally placed her arm around the girl and held her close. "I don't think so dear. And Nicole and I will do everything we can to make sure it doesn't happen," Sally said as she looked up into Nicole's eyes for reassurance.

"Absolutely. The very least we can do is make sure the newspapers get hold of this and tell each and every sordid little detail. It's probably time for some good old-fashioned calling on state representatives, county council, and senators, too. We don't want this swept under any rug. We don't want to leave any place for anyone, no matter how remotely or innocently involved in this obscene intrigue, to escape the glare of what I intend to turn into one rowdy media event," Nicole asserted vehemently as she clenched her fists. The physical motion of clenching her forgotten sprained wrist made a sharp pain course up her arm. She winced.

175

"That's all well and good, dear," Sally said as she put her hand around Nicole's good arm. "But we have a lot more to do right here, right now, and I think we ought to let the sheriff tend to his business and get you back to work here."

"OK," Nicole said, mollified. "It just makes me so angry. I hope they get the bastards and put them where they can't do anyone any harm ever again."

"I have every confidence in the sheriff," Sally soothed. "Now, I think you and I and Gwynn Marian ought to go see if we've got everything we need from the lumber company to fix the back of our home," Sally said as she steered her two women back toward the house.

Chapter 13
Bread & Roses

Gardening is not simply a spring and summer activity. Your garden will need attention throughout the year. A certain amount of preparation for winter is necessary as the growing season comes to a close, and some care endures to the hope of spring. The garden should be mulched to prevent excessive freezing and thawing with the likely harshness of the weather. With proper mulching, you will be rewarded with the continual harvest of freshly rooted vegetables throughout the long fall and much of the winter. Properly mulched, the garden soils will freeze little or not at all. In this manner, plant roots and soil organisms will have the opportunity to remain partly active during the winter and ensure early production when the spring returns.

Mounding is necessary for some shrubs and perennials. Mounding is done at the base of the plant to protect the root system. Shrubs should be cut back and then provided with a protective layer of mounding and mulch.

Biennials need to receive greater protection than the mulching and mounding recommended for shrubs and perennials. Cardboard or wooden boxes should be inverted over the tops of the biennials you wish to see again in spring. Mulch before covering.

A little care and preparation will provide you with a healthy and beautiful return as the year revolves to renewal once again.

Groundwork

Nicole and Sally sat in front of the fireplace and watched the bright flames dancing among the logs. Nicole sat on the davenport with Sally curled by her side and sighed contentedly to herself. Sally turned in Nicole's arms and reached up to touch the face of the woman she loved. Nicole wrapped her arms soothingly around Sally and held her close in the exchange of sweet kisses.

"If you persist," Nicole said, releasing Sally's lips

from her own, "you'll be in danger of me wanting you right here, right now."

"Can't have that, now can we? Gwynn Marian is supposed to be out riding her pony, but with the snow picking up, I don't know," Sally said, looking out the bay window over Nicole's shoulder. "She's likely to be heading back to the stalls and then here."

"There's nothing she doesn't know now," Nicole assured Sally. "But, intimacy between you and me, particularly the sort you're making me want and want right now, doesn't have to, shouldn't be, part of her awareness."

"I'm acutely aware of that," Sally said, snuggling into Nicole's arms. "I'm also aware that sitting here, as lovely as it is, is not getting things done. And we have a lot to prepare for."

"In due time, in due time," Nicole appeased. She knew where this conversation was going. She knew the work that she and Sally had started and how much was left to do.

"Time? It certainly took time for the insurance company to pay off on the restaurant and house. It took time for that little house we bought to get moved and set up on the old foundation. It took more time for the equipment and the River Market space lease. And it's taking time to promote the new cheesecakes and other organic foods business we're going to be building there," Sally huffed.

"That may be," Nicole consoled. "Just remember, though, you don't have to do it alone. Jake will run the storefront in the River Market. I think he's really looking forward to it. You and Martha will do the cheesecakes, herb oils, and vinegars, while your mother ramrods the shipping of food baskets for the organically inclined in a two-county area. Everything is at the ready. It will be fine," Nicole assured Sally.

"You really think so?"

"I know so. I even know more than that," Nicole said, pulling Sally closer. "I know your mother loves you; she's even managed to talk to me lately without looking like an oncoming storm cloud. I know your daughter loves you, but you know that, too. You certainly shouldn't be confused as to how I feel about you. I understand, too, that there's a lot of work to do, but even with that, I can't remember ever being happier. Although I'm a little confused," Nicole declared.

"About what, dear?" Sally asked in concern.

"Simply that, of all my mental meandering, fantasies, and speculations —" She hesitated, shaking her head and grinning.

"What, what's wrong?" Sally asked, sitting up and searching Nicole's face anxiously.

"I simply never imagined I'd ever be working on a farm again. I ran away from a farm better than twenty years ago. It feels strange to find myself here and to be very happily here and with you," Nicole puzzled.

"Oh, that. Then let's set the record straight, or rather just set the record, shall we?" Sally said, pulling Nicole to her. "You don't work here. You belong here, make no mistake about that. We own this together now. I wouldn't want to do it without you. As far as the other goes, it reminds me of something my father once told me."

"And what would that be," Nicole said as she nibbled Sally's neck.

"He told me that sometimes, no matter how far you go, what you think you're running from or reaching for, you're always coming home."

LOOKING FOR NAIAD?

Buy our books at
www.naiadpress.com

or call our toll-free number
1-800-533-1973

or by fax (24 hours a day)
1-850-539-9731

A few of the publications of
THE NAIAD PRESS, INC.
P.O. Box 10543   Tallahassee, Florida 32302
Phone (850) 539-5965
Toll-Free Order Number: 1-800-533-1973
Web Site: WWW.NAIADPRESS.COM
Mail orders welcome. Please include 15% postage.
Write or call for our free catalog which also features an
incredible selection of lesbian videos.

WINDROW GARDEN by Janet McClellan. 192 pp. They discover a passion they never dreamed possible.   ISBN 1-56280-216-X $11.95

PAST DUE by Claire McNab. 224 pp. 10th Carol Ashton mystery.   ISBN 1-56280-217-8   11.95

CHRISTABEL by Laura Adams. 224 pp. Two captive hearts and the passion that will set them free.   ISBN 1-56280-214-3   11.95

PRIVATE PASSIONS by Laura DeHart Young. 192 pp. An unforgettable new portrait of lesbian love . . .   ISBN 1-56280-215-1   11.95

BAD MOON RISING by Barbara Johnson. 208 pp. 2nd Colleen Fitzgerald mystery.   ISBN 1-56280-211-9   11.95

RIVER QUAY by Janet McClellan. 208 pp. 3rd Tru North mystery.   ISBN 1-56280-212-7   11.95

ENDLESS LOVE by Lisa Shapiro. 272 pp. To believe, once again, that love can be forever.   ISBN 1-56280-213-5   11.95

FALLEN FROM GRACE by Pat Welch. 256 pp. 6th Helen Black mystery.   ISBN 1-56280-209-7   11.95

THE NAKED EYE by Catherine Ennis. 208 pp. Her lover in the camera's eye . . .   ISBN 1-56280-210-0   11.95

OVER THE LINE by Tracey Richardson. 176 pp. 2nd Stevie Houston mystery.   ISBN 1-56280-202-X   11.95

JULIA'S SONG by Ann O'Leary. 208 pp. Strangely disturbing . . . strangely exciting.   ISBN 1-56280-197-X   11.95

LOVE IN THE BALANCE by Marianne K. Martin. 256 pp. Weighing the costs of love . . .   ISBN 1-56280-199-6   11.95

PIECE OF MY HEART by Julia Watts. 208 pp. All the stuff that dreams are made of —   ISBN 1-56280-206-2   11.95

MAKING UP FOR LOST TIME by Karin Kallmaker. 240 pp. Nobody does it better . . .   ISBN 1-56280-196-1   11.95

GOLD FEVER by Lyn Denison. 224 pp. By author of *Dream Lover.* ISBN 1-56280-201-1   11.95

WHEN THE DEAD SPEAK by Therese Szymanski. 224 pp. 2nd Brett Higgins mystery. ISBN 1-56280-198-8   11.95

FOURTH DOWN by Kate Calloway. 240 pp. 4th Cassidy James mystery. ISBN 1-56280-205-4   11.95

A MOMENT'S INDISCRETION by Peggy J. Herring. 176 pp. There's a fine line between love and lust . . . ISBN 1-56280-194-5   11.95

CITY LIGHTS/COUNTRY CANDLES by Penny Hayes. 208 pp. About the women she has known . . . ISBN 1-56280-195-3   11.95

POSSESSIONS by Kaye Davis. 240 pp. 2nd Maris Middleton mystery. ISBN 1-56280-192-9   11.95

A QUESTION OF LOVE by Saxon Bennett. 208 pp. Every woman is granted one great love. ISBN 1-56280-205-4   11.95

RHYTHM TIDE by Frankie J. Jones. 160 pp. . . . to desire passionately and be passionately desired. ISBN 1-56280-189-9   11.95

PENN VALLEY PHOENIX by Janet McClellan. 208 pp. 2nd Tru North Mystery. ISBN 1-56280-200-3   11.95

BY RESERVATION ONLY by Jackie Calhoun. 240 pp. A chance for true happiness. ISBN 1-56280-191-0   11.95

OLD BLACK MAGIC by Jaye Maiman. 272 pp. 9th Robin Miller mystery. ISBN 1-56280-175-9   11.95

LEGACY OF LOVE by Marianne K. Martin. 240 pp. Women will do anything for her . . . ISBN 1-56280-184-8   11.95

LETTING GO by Ann O'Leary. 160 pp. Laura, at 39, in love with 23-year-old Kate. ISBN 1-56280-183-X   11.95

LADY BE GOOD edited by Barbara Grier and Christine Cassidy. 288 pp. Erotic stories by Naiad Press authors. ISBN 1-56280-180-5   14.95

CHAIN LETTER by Claire McNab. 288 pp. 9th Carol Ashton mystery. ISBN 1-56280-181-3   11.95

NIGHT VISION by Laura Adams. 256 pp. Erotic fantasy romance by "famous" author. ISBN 1-56280-182-1   11.95

SEA TO SHINING SEA by Lisa Shapiro. 256 pp. Unable to resist the raging passion . . . ISBN 1-56280-177-5   11.95

These are just a few of the many Naiad Press titles — we are the oldest and largest lesbian/feminist publishing company in the world. We also offer an enormous selection of lesbian video products. Please request a complete catalog. We offer personal service; we encourage and welcome direct mail orders from individuals who have limited access to bookstores carrying our publications.